MW00592134

# Twenty Odd Tales
## *Including the Orinoco Stories*

by

## John Schoonbeek

Illustrated by Karen E. Gersch

# Twenty Odd Tales

Including the Orinoco Stories

by
John Schoonbeek

Photo: Jorge Santos

© 2011  by John Schoonbeck

Also by this author:

*My Father's Circus*
*( novel, 2009, 2012)*
Hudson House

*La Barranca (the Canyon)*
*with Jorge A.Santos*
*(stories and photographs, 2011)*
PoTown Press

*Dance for Dr .Notkin*
*(novel in progress)*

*Crisis, a Handbook for Systemic Intervention*
*with Jane. S. Ferber, M.D.*
Institute for Human Studies
*1977, 1983)*

ISBN:  978-1-58776-928-3

Library of Congress Number:  2012931831

# CONTENTS

## Part 1 : The Seceders

## Part 2: Orinoco Stories

## Part 3: The Law of Return

From Concert of Life Nobody Gets a Program

(Dutch/American Proverb)

*Acknowledgments*

Drawings by
**KAREN E. GERSCH**
*artbykeg.info*

Tales in *Part 2: Orinoco Stories,* with drawings by
**Nicholas Schoonbeck**
reprinted with permission of
*Friends Journal, © 1988-89* and
*Upriver/Downriver Magazine*


Editing and Design:
Roger Hellman
*Hudson House*


*Photos by Jorge Santos*

For Leslie Johnson
and
Sage Profita-Schoonbeck

# The Seceders' New Shoes

Great Grandma Gorehouse was a short person, but strong and compact as a small accordion. Her husband, known to us only as Mr. Gorehouse, helped her raise their five daughters on milk from the cows grazing on their little farm near Ada, Michigan. Once a week Great Grandma baked five loaves of bread. Her flour was ground from the winter wheat and rye that she had sown and reaped herself.

When the couple first arrived from Holland, both sixteen years of age, they went to the Dutch enclave near Ada, settling down on a piece of land that resembled their polders in Holland: flat, sandy, where they could watch high white clouds rolling in overhead from the Great Lake to the west.

Mr. Gorehouse, thin and weak-looking as he was, knew how to nail up a simple house and a barn, so they soon kept cows and hens there, and dug a garden to grow red potatoes and fat green leeks for making *huts-pot*.

A year after the birth of their first daughter, Trintje, a second girl was born. Then three more girls followed, one more every year. The five sisters grew up happy on the farm, keeping to Dutch ways at home, which satisfied their mother, but learning American habits at school, which pleased their Father more. Trintje was to be the first to receive an American school diploma, which made her very unpopular at home.

All the girls were at school, unawares, on the day in early November that Mr. Gorehouse suddenly died. He had come down with influenza the day before, and in the morning his wife had not wanted to disturb him but he lay so still that she finally realized that he was dead. By the time the girls walked home from school that afternoon, Great Grandma had already dug a grave in the sandy soil behind the barn.

Trintje, the eldest daughter, was perhaps the most affected by their father's passing, but she was also the most practical, much like her mother. She took charge of the corpse on the bed. Poor Mr. Gorehouse lay with the weight of two large American pennies now keeping his eyelids closed. "At least he didn't die with his mouth open," Trintje said. "It's hard to get it closed again when that happens." Her mother nodded. Trintje knew what she was thinking. They rolled the edges of his blanket in to make it into a litter, and then, with twelve hands of varying sizes grasping the rolled edges, the women carried the corpse out and lowered it in with rope, below frost line, safe from digging animals. It was a simple funeral. They prayed, they sang a hymn. Amen.

Early death was a pretty frequent occurrence in those days. There was no question that the young women would stay to labor with their mother on the farm. "Steady on," had always been her command, words that would echo in the family for generations afterward.

And life did go on. Passers-by always found the young women out in the field, cultivating the crops. "Work!" the girls sang, "for the night is coming!" Great Grandma, who neither sang nor spoke in English, sometimes smiled as she worked beside her girls. She herself was so hale and strong that the girls bragged to their friends that they were sure she'd finish her life without ever having to see a doctor.

But, of course, just as the hymn warned, there did come a day years later when that certainty weakened. The old woman woke up one morning unable to walk upon her right foot. The girls, though nearly grown, were terrified, never having considered that something could happen to Mother.

Now, we should mention here that back in the Netherlands Great Grandma had always worn wooden shoes, and as you might expect she kept on wearing them after coming to America on the boat. The hand-carved *klompen* were practical for farm work. You slipped them on going from the house across the muddy barnyard, and you just stepped out and left them on the stoop when you went back indoors in your stockings. No soiled fingers.

But over the years, as Great Grandma noticed her Holland-born daughters dressing more like American women, she realized they were embarrassed by her wooden shoes, so she decided to switch to a pair of the leather American type.

The daughters' own leather footwear had been crafted by a Dutch cobbler in the nearby city of Grand Rapids, and that's where they all went, all six. The old woman had agreed, thinking it was likely that this cobbler would know about feet because he himself was lame.

Respectfully the young man measured her feet, then they sat and watched as he expertly cut the lasts, sewed the uppers, tried them, and before the day was done was able to wrap her new high-button leather shoes into a parcel of brown paper tied with string for her to carry home.

As soon as they were home Great Grandmother put the shoes on by herself, but she was obviously vexed at having to ask Trintje to tie up the laces. Still she smiled as she began walking back and forth, only occasionally having to grasp the back of a chair, like a Dutch child learning to ice skate.

Trintje looked on approvingly. All seemed to have gone pretty well. But as the days passed, Trintje began to sense that something was not exactly right. Maybe there was a misfit? Or her mother was not taking the shoes off at night?

11

Was she too proud to ask for help to tie them next day? But Trintje kept quiet, until the morning she found her mother sitting disconsolate on the edge of the bed, staring down at her right foot. She wouldn't speak. She couldn't stand up.

Trintje was not going to take any chances with her mother's health. She set off at once down the road to fetch the young Dutch doctor they knew from church. With no patients waiting in his office, (there seldom were any) he was willing to come to the farm, he said, if Trintje would ride with him in his carriage to show him where it was. She declined, thinking he knew very well where the farm was, but he refused to go if he had to drive while she walked. Finally, of course, she consented, stepping up to sit quietly and closely beside him the seven miles back. She didn't mind the ride at all.

Luckily, the doctor had also come from their own province of Groningen, because it took a Bible verse in that dialect to convince his patient to let him examine her foot. No man, including her late husband, had ever seen any part of Great Grandma's body exposed, nor had she herself ever seen a doctor up close. But she had to relent because the cows, coming in from pasture, were letting it be known they needed to be milked. She had to get the examination over with.

And so there in the parlor, with all pretending not to stare, the doctor gently worked the shoe off, and then, to Great Grandma's utter dismay, removed her black stocking as well.

He inspected the tiny naked foot, carefully moving the ankle this way and that, finally declaring that he could discern nothing wrong. The bones and joints were fine, he said. There were no bunions or lesions. Then he picked up the shoe itself and felt inside, and at last, with a triumphant smile, drew out a large metal shoehorn.

12

# How The Ramona Got Her Name

You may be wondering, from the way stories go, whether Trintje didn't go on to marry that Doctor from Groningen, but she did not. It's true that he had awakened something in her already restless young soul, and she did continue taking trips with the doctor in his carriage into the city of Grand Rapids on some pretext or other. But once there, she always went off on her own. People talked. In Holland it was the boys who roamed, not the girls. Eventually, it became known to all but her mother that it was not the doctor she favored at all: she was secretly seeing an older man who'd come from the horrible village of Staphorst!

Nowadays – a hundred years later - if you were to come upon the Dutch village of Staphorst you'd see nothing horrible about it. You'd find the same brick houses still roofed with thatch. Colorfully painted furniture is still made by hand, as are the textiles for the people's traditional dress.

Dairy cows are so beloved in Staphorst that the barn is attached to the kitchen, with no wall between, so in winter the cows stand right there like kitchen radiators, helping the peat stoves keep the house warm. Everything is very practical in Staphorst, a quality much admired in Holland. However there are other qualities of Staphorsters that are not so revered.

They – we - are a long-lived people, who want little to do with the rest of the world. If you happen to go there on Sabbath they might throw rocks at you, or confiscate your camera. It's the only village in Europe still listed as a health risk by the U.N. because the residents there refuse vaccines, and as a consequence have hosted deadly polio epidemic.

Staphorst may look like a Breughel painting, but, like a Breughel, what's charming at first glance becomes less so upon closer scrutiny. Many inhabitants have an odd inbred look, because Staphorsters tend not to marry outside their village. They hew to an extreme Calvinist sect that has been holding the fort since the invasion of the Spanish Armada. Everyone in Staphorst still goes twice to church, which brings up in Hollanders the unavoidable subject of undergarments, as the women of Staphorst wear no underwear on Sunday. The sermons last four hours, you see, and the women want to be able to rush out to pee on the grass and then rush back into church quickly, so as not to miss too much of the Word.

But everyone in Holland knows another story about the red and blue Staphorst women's underwear that opens from the front. People used to understand it as a means of saying that maids were there principally for "farmer's convenience." But we Staphorst apologists sometimes gave the economic explanation, which goes as follows:

Land has always been scarce and precious in Holland. Farmers who owned it didn't want to sire more than one or two children by their wives because they wanted no quarrels over inheritance that might result in having to one day divide the family's parcel.

But at the same time every farmer needed some strong young people around to work, so he had sex with the hired farm maids in the fields in order to produce the future laborers who'd never become legal heirs because they were

14

bastards. Farm maids were expected to be available for breeding with the farmers they worked for at all times. The easy-opening red and blue underwear was for "The Farmer's Convenience." It was also a symbol of their station.

My grandfather Jan Achter, the older Staphorst man who was eventually to meet and marry Trintje in Grand Rapids, was born to such a farm maid. It made him a skeptical person. He knew that in Holland his kind would never do anything but serve. In one of his jokes a Dutch banker toasts a preacher: You keep the people stupid, and I'll keep them broke. *"Houdt u ze maar dom, ik houdt ze wel arm."*

Let me interject here that I visited this village of my grandfather many decades later. On the strength of my looks, which is to say I looked like every other twenty year old in the village, I'd been introduced to a man named Vloedgraven, a man nearly 100 years of age, who remembered my grandpa from their boyhood. Without doing the math I asked him to show me where my family had lived. He was willing to take me there but I had no bicycle, so he insisted I ride on the back of his, to the old Achter house.

Neighbors laughed as we rode by, an upright, nearly-hundred year old man briskly pedaling, while behind on the baggage rack slouched an apparently lazy youth, legs just dangling, who looked like he'd been born right there in the village. Mr. Vloedgraven was amused too. Clearly he had done it on purpose.

We stopped at an empty field. "That was the Achter house," he said with a gesture. "The Germans blew it up in World War Two. But it was just the same as my house. Let's go back, I'll show you how it looked." We rode back and went into his thatch roofed house to sit down to a tiny glass of genever as he explained to me many things.

In the photo above, the small low window behind Mr. Vloedgraven is for a room called the Opkamer. All farms with daughters had one of these special girl bedrooms, built over the root cellar, with that small, low window without hinges, which was left open at night so boys could enter. After a girl was pregnant and proved fertile, a marriage would be arranged by her father, though not necessarily with the night visitor. Most old Staphorsters were conceived this way: through "venster vryen," window love.

Now, the Staphorst man Trintje had met in Grand Rapids was Jan Klaas Achter, whose own father had left him and the family in order to secede from the church. Nobody was sorry, I was told, when he left Staphorst. (Seceders had to leave town, because Dutch villages only allowed the existence of one big church, precisely to prevent secessions.) But as economic times had worsened more young people had taken to preaching heresies at night from the back of farm wagons, and some left for America to open their own congregations.

One night Old Jan the Elder simply walked off like that, leaving his son, my grandfather Jan Klaas, to provide for the family. He was fifteen when he took over his father's job, delivering bread for the Hekman baker family, using a dogcart in summer, a canal sled in winter. Along the bread route he was apparently able to find enough loose time to sire a child through vinster vryen, but there was never any agreement between the families about making a marriage. So eventually when money came by mail from a church in America, young Jan put Staphorst behind him too, and sailed on a ship called the Maasdam to New York. From there he took a train to Michigan, where he met Grandma Trintje in a bowling alley.

For his first years in America, Jan Klaas worked the land that his father had rented, and he also hired himself out to other farms, secretly saving dollars for marriage. By the time he met Trintje in Grand Rapids he had gathered over a hundred dollars, which he kept hidden in a clay jar in the root cellar of his father's farm. One day when Jan Klaas had gone to town the old man found the jar and stole the money. He also stole and sold Jan Klaas's pet ducks, to get even more money so that he could buy a cow.

Trintje was disgusted to learn that her wedding would be postponed, and she never forgave it, but she knew Jan Klaas was a Staphorst boy. His family had to have cows. Their own cows on their own land. Then he'd be able to leave.

I once asked my own Aunt Helen, the maiden aunt who kept the family history, if my grandparents Jan and Trintje might have met through "venster-vryen." Aunt Helen

17

was shocked that I had learned the term. No, she said, Jan had loved Trintje so much that he'd smuggled her out of Staphorst hidden in a butter churn. Aunt Helen didn't realize I already knew that the bride and groom had come in different years from different towns on different boats, and that Trintje had never set foot in Staphorst nor would she ever have done so in daylight.

Here is Grandma Trintje, fourth from left. As you can see, the sisters were inseparable, til American life pulled them asunder.

And yes, that's Great Grandmother Gorehouse, herself, on the left. Note that she lists to starboard.

The daughters of Jan Klaas and Trintje, (my Mom, Marion, and my aunts, Grace and Helen,) knew little of their parents' story, nor did they care to know more. They said the parents always spoke in "that old Dutch" which the girls didn't understand and didn't want to. 'Pappy' wanted them to be Americans, anyway. He drove his Detroit-made cars with the stars and stripes flying, and he smoked cigars like an American tycoon, still wearing his Dutch Staphorster cap. He didn't know that people whispered that the first of his three daughters, Grace, had really been a result of venster vryen by a different father. They knew how those Staphorsters were.

Helen (L) would spend her long life with a group of women friends called The Naughty Niners. She taught first grade to more than half the people living in Grand Rapids, even helping her own "Pappy" learn English. Here's an example of a letter he wrote to my Mom in 1943, the year I was born:

> *My dear Eaglet - I bet you thought I was forgeting you but not so I been putting off writing so many times so I thouth to nite I would sit down I do this hard struggle well Dear I hope this will find you in a good moode. You know this was the first Xmas you were not here and top it off Dickey was sick so I was pretty blu but did not let on.*
>
> *The poots (pooch) got a new bed now, mother put a rug before the ridestre (register) for Rowdy. I see in the paper the war is going to be over they sure have them on the run lets hope all the boys can go home well Marion I don't know much news will write soon again yours      Pappy*

Grandpa's life had taken him from a Staphorst farm across the sea to farm, and then to work in the furniture factories of America, where he built his own house, raised his three daughters, and lived to see his grandchildren. I had the honor to be part of his life during the 1940s. At the factory, during the day, he carved billiard tables. In the summer, when it was too hot for people to go bowling, he also worked nights sanding and varnishing bowling lanes by hand. He loved the game, once bowling a perfect 300. His picture was in the newspaper. Everyone said it was his crowning achievement.

But being a Grandpa myself now, I know that his real crowning glory was to be able to claim several surviving grandchildren. Grandpa Jan is why I, the oldest, am named John, and why I go sit in the barn when I'm mad, and why I keep poultry and do carpentry. It's why I've built four of my own houses, and five seaworthy boats.

Though Pappy died before I was old enough to know truly him, I do remember him setting me in his lap and opening the Grand Rapids Press to read – in his odd English – the serial stories of Uncle Wiggily Longears, the Rabbit Gentleman. Oh the house smelled of lilac water and newspaper ink, and my grandma's warm bread tasted so good, and all was well with the world in those days. And once in a while, Grandpa would take me car riding, as he had done with his daughters.

One trip I will never forget was the day he drove me to Reed's Lake, where we went on a paddlewheel steamboat, named the Ramona. Pappy told me, as we looked over the side, of how he had once sailed over flooded villages and seen the water dogs and water pigs and heard the drowned bells tolling when, as a boy, he sailed upon the Zuider Zee.

And now, I hope my granddaughter Sage knows why there was such a far-away look in my eye when she and I launched the first boat we built, and why I named it the Ramona. I had waited half a century to build a vessel that we could sail back down the Hudson to New York, where our Dutch ancestors once disembarked, and if the boat was stout enough to carry all my dreams, we'd even sail east from there, into the Atlantic, all the way back to Staphorst.

# The Cobbler Shop

During the same turn into the 20th Century when Jan met Trintje, there was another Dutch family growing up three blocks away. The progenitor of that family, Albert Jacob Berends Schoonbeek, was the cobbler who had assembled Great Grandma's shoes. A stern but acquiescent man, he would be my other great grandfather.

When still a small child in the very far north coast of Holland, Albert had nearly died from infection after his bare foot was crushed under a horse's hoof. He had gone on with life optimistically, as the young will do, walking with a stick. But not until he was an adolescent did he get real shoes, because none of the local carvers had been able to make a shoe to fit his misshapen foot. So finally he carved his own.

The shoes came out so well, and the boy's courage was so admired, that other villagers decided he was predestined to be a shoe carver, because we don't choose our professions – in the right order of things, we wait expectantly, and are chosen to do certain work. We will be given our sign and our task.

Albert might have prospered at his trade, but few people then had money to buy even wooden shoes. A potato famine throughout Europe had all but shut down Dutch commerce. Men from the village of Termunten were leaving for the Dutch colonies like Java. A few of Albert's close neighbors, seceding from their church, were deciding to sail instead to "Michigan," where they knew they'd find more religious fanatics, not to mention more potatoes.

These 'Seceders' like the Staphorsters before them, left the village one family at a time, until months later letters arrived and it became known that they were prospering. In Michigan they built dark red brick churches  and then sent letters back to Termunten offering one-way ship passage to any men willing to come over to join the new congregations.

I'm not sure that my Great Grandpa Albert as a boy of fifteen really had any strong feelings about the Heidelberg Cathechism or the Belgic Confession, or maybe he did, but he certainly knew a free ticket when he saw one, and might even have been thinking there'd be plenty of shoes to carve over in Michigan for the many Dutch emigrants. So, tenderly young, crippled, and alone, he set out from Termunten on the peat paths beside the canals. Because he was cheerful, he was often able to trade work for passage on canal schouwes until he reached Rotterdam.

It was a busy port. Having very few guilders in his pocket but a day to wait, he decided to avoid the crowded rooming houses that raged with cholera, and instead went directly aboard the docked ship, the Atalanta, which was in the process of stowing for each passenger five pounds of bread, two of salted meat, some coffee, rice, groats, a pound each of flour, beans and peas, and ten pounds of potatoes. He was also given several "oranges," a fruit he'd heard of but never seen. Biting into an orange that first evening, he found it alarmingly sour. A young woman to whom he had offered another of his three oranges smiled at his puckers and winces, explaining that the fruit were actually called lemons, to be eaten only at mid-voyage to avoid scurvy. They couldn't stop laughing about it together. In fact they kept on laughing, hardly minding the long, grey, miserable voyage.

The girl, Gretje, had been given a cabin, but Albert crossed the heaving sea in steerage - outdoor deck class - on that listing, leaking sailing vessel ballasted by a dead coal engine ostensibly there for use against the winds from the west. Not until nine sick weeks had passed did they arrive at Castle Garden, New York, where immigration police separated the men from the women.

Albert said farewell to his new girlfriend, and went ashore to find the steam train to Grand Rapids, where, once the locomotive huffed to a stop a day and night later, he harkened to the sound of his fellow immigrants klop-klopping like horses down the concrete train platform in their wooden shoes, headed for the furniture factories, where they intended to start work that very same day.

The only thing that Albert didn't know, of course, was that those same Dutch travelers, even Gretje, the young woman on the boat who he would later meet again and marry, were going to use their first paychecks in the new land to buy leather American shoes. Because more than anything they didn't want to be stared at and mocked as Dutch immigrants.

People tell me now that Albert wasn't a person who liked to indulge in disappointment. With the help of the church's charity he set up a cobbler shop and learned to make leather shoes for the Dutchmen who continued to arrive. On his profits, minus ten percent, Albert and his wife raised their only son Ben, who would grow up to become a US Mail letter-carrier in Grand Rapids, driving a horse wagon, the doors of its black enameled cabin painted with gilt letters.

Ben the mailman married young, and sired four children, of whom the middle two died. The last baby, and thus the last grandchild of old Albert and Gretje, was my own father...Bernard, (for Berends.)

Dad changed his name to Earl as he grew up to be a deugenits – a no-good. By the age of fifteen, he was drinking, chasing women, and playing the banjo.

24

Great Grandpa Albert, the cripple from Holland, still lived when this last grandson was born, but he never heard him play the banjo. The old cobbler had become reclusive by that time, and he died alone, in predestined penury. Along life's way he had shed or hidden his probably Jewish middle names, Jacob and Berends, but they lived on with my father. The stones back in the Jewish cemetery in Termunten, old as the Inquisition itself, might have told the whole tale to those of us who went seeking, but the Germans also blew up that cemetery along with the most of the town in World War II.

Could old Albert have really been part Jewish? I had grown up watching his son, my Grandpa Ben, reading the Dutch Bible several hours each day, rocking back and forth like a davenning Rabbi, moving his lips. Neither he nor his wife would cook or turn on the lights on Sabbath, nor eat shellfish. Yet they were ardent Christians. Did Grandpa Ben davven without knowing why? Did they keep to Jewish laws and customs out of habit? Because it was what their ancestors had done?

Of course, Old Albert could also have lost a Jewish name, as many did, at the port of entry. It could even have been expunged at his death by the Grand Rapids Press. Their obituary just said that Albert Schoonbeek, (and here the obit gave the address of a rooming house on the wrong end of Wealthy Street) had died of cirrhosis. They published things like that in Grand Rapids in those days. And judging from the kind of indignant right wing politicians the town has produced in the century since then, I'd imagine they still do.

# In a Pear Tree

My parents were both born at home on dining room tables, Mom from the womb of Trintje the farm girl, and Dad from that of Jennie, the wife of Ben the mailman. The houses they were born in were only three blocks apart, but the families had come from different provinces and different religious opinions, so they never had any reason to be acquainted. The Schoonbeek family had boys, the Achters girls. As kids, Mom and Dad passed each other daily on the sidewalk. She walked south to the public school, and he walked north toward the Christian Reformed Academy to read scripture. By high school they were carefully timing their morning walks so as to be sure of ignoring each other as they passed each day.

Grandma Trintje had long since married Jan Klaas of Staphorst and had moved from the farm into the city of Grand Rapids. Great Grandma Gorehouse, grown deaf in her last years, left the world soon after a new tar road divided her farmland. Crossing one morning in order to get to her cow pasture, she was struck by an oncoming coal truck she had not heard, and hurled forty feet to a bewildered and agonizing death. I don't know if the five daughters buried her with the hated leather shoes on, but as soon as she was in the ground beside Mr. Gorehouse, Trintje packed up for Grand Rapids.

Trintje was proud of having found a husband, but was a little embarrassed, too, that he came from the notorious Dutch village of Staphorst, where she'd been told the full-skirted, bonneted women wore no underwear on Sabbath because sermons lasted four hours, and a woman who had to go out to pee on the grass wanted to do it quickly, so as to rush back in without missing too much of the Word. She thought it seemed very practical. For them.

Trintje was not pleased when her husband went back to traditional Staphorst attire, and as her own daughters grew up they were embarrassed too. Trintje was forever calling attention to his peasant dress, comparing it to the giant pearls and Groningen clothes she had herself affected. Now she was high class. "Staphorst," she would recite teasingly from a Dutch ditty, "is ein Stink-nest."

Though I recall her scorn for the Staphorsters and I can still hear her hoots at the mention of the savage Frisians (people from the province next to hers,) I mostly remember my Grandma Trintje in the kindness of her old age, her gold teeth and lilac scent; I still see her with a rubber garden hose, sprinkling the thin pale grass that grew out of the Michigan sand to be raked like hair.

Later naming herself Tressa, (discarding the name Trintje along with her wooden shoes,) she learned she had found an ambitious partner in Jan Klaas. At first working as an assistant to a Dutch neighbor who was carving owls for the Supreme Court's benches, he soon graduated to billiard tables. He also built, with hand tools, his own house, at the edge of the city where the family could get horse-cart delivery of bottled milk. They could even order coal delivered for the cellar furnace. Tressa loved the luxury. And with all that, they were still never very far from the kindly smell of other people's cows, grazing down the hill from where they lived.

The day they married, John and Tressa planted a pear tree in the back yard. By the time their little Grace, Helen and Marion in that descending order were old enough to climb it, the tree had also grown stout enough to hold them. They went aloft to spy all round and all the way down to the rail crossing where the trains passed six times a day.

And as more years passed and the pear tree grew ever stronger, the girls got more reticent about climbing it, until each reached the day she'd climb it not at all. There might be boys around who would look up, so it was not from the treetop but from their second floor room, with its curtained windows, mirrors, and the smell of bath powder, that the maturing girls would lie and dream of the prowling boys, and listen for the far sound of the train whistle and rumble of endless freight cars on rainy nights as the century moved on.

# Kabouters

I tell my own granddaughter now that in the Dutch immigrant world into which I was born there were no malls, no classes of folk called "consumers," "celebrities," or "the homeless," although sure, we bought things, there were movie stars, and we had a few summer hobos and gypsies camping down by Plaster Creek. We kids were never allowed to go down there except in winter for sledding, long after the gypsies had gone away... gone, according to Grandma, with stolen Dutch children in the back of their wagons. In my dreams I was one of the snatched.

We had kabouters, too, which my father called Spying Gnomes, pronounced gunOmees. These were very tiny people, seldom seen, about eight inches tall, who kept to themselves but watched and judged, severely, everything we did. The soles of their shoes were carved in the form of bird feet so they could walk around freely, leaving only bird tracks. The GunOmees, sadly, were often carried away and eaten by crows. I tried to get back at the evil birds by stalking them in my Grandma's back yard, being allowed to do this only on condition that I catch them by shaking salt on their tails. I never caught one, but almost did, hundreds of times. I thought I might even catch a spying gunOmee too, by accident, of course.

Thankfully we didn't have computers in those days, nor television, and not even any fast food, There was, though, a place called Meijers' Hotdogs and Root Beer. Maybe six years after my father had moved me and my mom out of Grand Rapids and down to Ohio, one of my aunts back in

Michigan took a job at Meijers as a carhop. When we made our trip back once a year, the first thing my Mom wanted to do was to roll into Meijers, to see her sister slaving.

Aunt Grace, the oldest, had taken the carhop job only because her husband, a bad film maker, sat at home all day. Each morning Aunt Grace bobby-pinned her paper hat to her hair, and went off to trudge for hours carrying icy mugs of root beer and piles of warm hotdogs rolled in wax paper. "Ooh, be careful," my mother would say as Grace hung the cantilevered tray on the car window. 'I think you spilled some of my root beer! But that's okay."

Over in the shotgun seat, delicately nipping at her hot dog, Mom spoke from the privacy of her own world, unaware that both Aunt Grace and the middle sister Aunt Helen, still secretly referred to her as "Queenie." But I knew.

Whatever my mom came out with, Aunt Grace would just stoop and smile through the car window. "Oh Marion how nice you look. Do you kids want anything else?" and she'd wipe her hands on her apron and go back to the kitchen still smiling because Dutch aunts never show defeat, they just sail on like frigates.

Our mother Marion, the youngest of the three sisters, was also said to be prettiest. She married Dad a few months after he enlisted for the war. They were wed a long train ride away, at Fort Polk, Louisiana, just days before his medical battalion embarked for the beaches of Normandy, where everything was getting under way.

Dad didn't come back to Grand Rapids until years after that, when he met, for the first time, really, his four year-old son: me. He had not been told I was born backward, half-strangling on the umbilicus and nearly killing my mother in the process, but he must have guessed that something had happened because she bore the scars on her belly, along with

30

many other scars, for the rest of her life. But then again, maybe she managed to hide it all somehow, like Great Grandma from Groningen.

Once the war was over, Dad moved Mom and me down to Ohio, where an army friend had found him a job selling carpets. He bought a small brick bungalow on the GI Bill, and they filled it with hope and love and a lot of carved mahogany Grand Rapids furniture.

Dad had a knack for selling rugs, so he made some money. He liked coming home to a neighborhood with other vets, too. We had crepe paper bike parades on Decoration Day, half-inflated balloons tied to our bike frame to rumble like motors on the spokes. We had big public Easter egg hunts, where certain eggs would win a live baby rabbit or duck.

Mom was a dutiful wife and a good mother, but after her second pregnancy, the delirious happiness re-formed into something much heavier in our new family. Mom went to the hospital to give birth to my brother Stephen, and he died a few days after he was born. Nobody knew why. People didn't have so many reasons back then, so many explanations for everything. He just died. I never even saw him.

I remember being taken to see the grave, though, layered with red and yellow leaves. At home, Stephen's never-wrinkled baby shoes, now cast in bronze, were set atop the piano beside my old worn ones. My mother no longer tried to conceal her despair. She left me on my own quite a bit from then on.

Dad dealt with it by staying out on the road, and he often came back drunk. Twice a year, though, he drove her back to Michigan, so she could put on confident airs for her sister at the hot dog stand, and show me off like a trick pony to Grandma and Aunt Helen. Still, the look on her face by then was subtly that of a crazy woman. In a way, she was already gone. Mom's heyday was over.

Ah, the road home to Michigan. I can still see the carsick race of passing telephone lines and poles, and hear the alert called out whenever someone saw a sequential poem coming up on a string of roadside Burma Shave signs:

Her Chariot
Raced 80 Per
They Hauled Away
What Had
Ben Her.

*Burma Shave*

\* \* \*

# Speaker Of The House

By the time I grew into a size ten, the piano was no longer just a showcase for bronzed baby shoes; my father had begun playing again and was teaching me chord progressions. I made a stamp collection and also invented a way to haul myself into a tree by sitting in a tin bushel roped through a pulley on a high branch, but once up there I didn't know how to get down, a pattern that would follow me throughout life.

Back in Michigan, Meier's Root Beer closed, which seemed impossible when I heard the news, but Aunt Grace had nevertheless enjoyed a change of fortune, as sometimes happens to the cheerful and resolute: her luckless filmmaker husband had stumbled into the new world of black and white television and was making commercials for clients as big as the Ionia Free Fair. He was making money.

My mother, who had stuck it out in our bungalow down in Silverton, Ohio, finally got pregnant again and gave birth to my handsome brother Phil, and then two years later to our happy, fabulous new sister, Leslie. There was joy in our family again. But Dad still drank.

Aunt Grace also gave birth somewhere along the line then, and she too lost her son. Dickie died at around the age of five. We always saw his baby photo, stood up on tables or on pianos in all the houses. They said he'd died because of the parents' blood types. And Grace just went on.

You see, we Dutch Seceders from Grand Rapids believe everything is predestined, so we simply go on and see what's next. Aunt Grace adopted herself a baby girl, and then she joined the art society and a weekly women's bridge group whose members included her long-time neighbor Betty Ford, who no one dreamed would one day become the First Lady of the United States and then go with work of her own that would prove even more consequential.

In fact all three sisters – Grace, Helen, and Marion – had also known Betty's husband, Gerald. He was in the same graduating class at South High as our Mom. Note that we always say he had been in her class, not she in his, because she never thought much of him, even as he rose in politics. For one thing, he was a Republican, which was no virtue in my mother's estimation. "I don't understand how he can be Speaker of the House," she'd say. It was the only thing in life that perplexed her, and she mentioned it often with the understanding that one of us would then ask "Why?" so she could reply "He was always so dumb."

Much later in life, when I'd been out in the world, I challenged her with something I'd heard at a dinner attended by Harold Lasswell, the father of political sociology, who'd been an advisor to all the recent Presidents. Lasswell told me that Gerald Ford was the most intelligent of all the Presidents, and that the smartest thing he ever did was act dumb. Mom just dismissed that idea, saying that Harold Lasswell must be pretty dumb himself.

There did come a time, though, many years after Gerry Ford's star had risen, when we all had to prevail upon Mom to call upon her acquaintance with him.

It was in the draft era of the Vietnam War, and some army brass had ignored my brother's application to serve his time as a conscientious objector. Our father had carried ambulance litters, not arms, in World War II, even in the Battle of the Bulge where he'd got a field commission and a Bronze Star for valor. He carried dead and wounded, but he never carried a gun. And I'd been a conscientious objector too, during the Vietnam War, doing two years of civilian hospital service instead of fighting. Mom had always kept silent on the subject of Objection.

She was also silent when we pleaded with her to put in a call to then-House Speaker Ford to help our brother get out when the army had refused to even read his application to do alternative service. Her reluctance seemed so odd at the time, but when I thought about it years later, about the interaction between her and Dad when the topic came up, I thought maybe in high school Mom and Gerry Ford had known each other better than any of us would have assumed, and maybe she didn't want Ford (or Dad) to think that she was really calling for some other motive, or that there could be risk of rekindling. I never dared ask her about that.

She did call The Speaker of the House, finally, when nobody else was around, and in a few days our brother was discharged from the army. Mom sounded resigned about it when she called me the day Phil got home, but there was discontent concealed in her voice, as if he had gotten away with cheating, and I remember saying to myself she probably gave him a hug but still burnt the spaghetti. She had her ways.

# The Sch Of Scheveningen

Our ways, of course, were Dutch ways. Memory of the Netherlandish wars figured heavily and invisibly in all of our family history. My father sometimes referred to the defeat of the Spanish Armada to explain Dutch religious schisms in Grand Rapids Michigan. I was not allowed to ride in a Volkswagen due to World War II, and was told to be proud of having a name like Schoonbeek, a name so Dutch that it was near impossible for Germans to pronounce. It's the sound of the "Sch." Dutch soldiers used to detect German spies in the war by asking them for the best Dutch beach resort. (Answer: Scheveningen.)

So, with all of us having been born in the ethnic Dutch community of western Michigan, I'm not sure why, after the war, my father moved us down into the German communities of the Ohio River valley. We were immigrants again.

Dad stopped calling himself Earl, going on the road instead as "Bernie," hoping the rug-store owners would think he was "of the Hebrew faith," as he sanctimoniously put it, and buy only from him. It worked, up to a point, but who knows what they said to each other after he left?

Of course this was 1940s America, where everyone aspired to look and be Just Regular, as my father would say. Everyone ate all meals at table, said grace, proper manners, dinner at noon, supper at five. Mom specialized in Tuna Delight-Deluxe, Metwurst and potatoes, Corn-Hamburg medley, and pot roast with carrots leeks and potatoes mashed up (hutspot.) On rare occasions we had dark green beans sprinkled with stark white navy beans, a dish called, in Dutch, "naked children in the grass."

At night, Dad made Graveyard Stew, white soda crackers broken into white milk. His father Ben used to warn that with food, white was the color of death. So Dad invented graveyard stew to spite him, and did some slurping and trembling while eating it.

At night after dinner we children went outside by ourselves to play kick the can under the single streetlight, creeping in like tigers toward the only pool of light. We were free to go anywhere we wanted, day or night, and we walked miles to school, alone or in groups, from first grade on. Life was safe. At night we'd only come in when our mothers called from the front stoop. Each mom had her distinctive call, our Mom's "kyudeling"the most embarrassing.

In summer I kept to the porches and backyards with the neighborhood girls. We played canasta, put on talent or magic shows, walked on stilts. We held fundraising carnivals to buy Iron Lungs for children with polio. There were no vaccines then. We fully expected to get polio ourselves, from swimming, and we all knew of someone who had it.

The world was our museum and garden, we found fossils, trilobites, arrowheads, and salamanders; we watched hummingbirds, grew violets, jack in the pulpits, and roses. At night there were lightning bugs to catch in glass jars, because there were lots of fields and woods and uninhabited places that seemed to belong to no one. We went barefoot.

In fact, the world itself was not entirely discovered then. Out there on the continents were unclimbed peaks, undescended rivers, uncontacted tribes, and even uncharted waters. And so we grew up in a world of possibility, with the expectation that some day we too could go forth, and perhaps discover something.

*Drawings by Nicholas Schoenhoff*

# PART 2
# Orinoco Stories

# Into the River Delta

*(1994, from a never-sent letter to my son, who said I had never told him the truth about my life.)*

Dear Son,

  I'm starting this long-promised letter to you in the airport while waiting for a night flight to Caracas and from there into the Orinoco Delta. I'd hoped I'd be exploring those waters some day aboard our own little Ramona, maybe with you at the helm, but I never counted on your growing up, having a family of your own, never expected you to hate boats, so I'm taking a plane into the unknown by myself, knowing that just as I couldn't have built the boat without you, I couldn't sail it alone either.

  The inevitable separation between father and son is so painful. I think the last thread of childhood connection between us actually broke while we were building the Ramona, when it was time to turn her right side up and you brought your brawny friends over to help manage the unwieldy weight of the leaden keel.

  From the beginning I think you and I saw the whole project differently, don't you? For me the boat was going to be a way I could sail away with you, away from danger. But for you the boat was more like the thing that was going to make me go away for good. Remember when you smashed the scale model I'd made before we built it? Guess I should have noticed.

But there we all were, tense, edgy inside the hot tin storage shed, the hull upside down before us on sawhorses, four hundred pound lead keel uppermost. We had to turn it over. Your friends started getting loud and raucous, and suddenly on your own, as if wanting to get it done and get out of there, you and the other boys lifted the boat up, against my protests, we lost control, and the huge thing revolved around itself by gravity and crashed onto the floor, breaking some boards, but thankfully nobody's foot bones.

Yeah, I was angry, even though it was an accident. I should have realized that the broken boards revealed where the boat's weaknesses were, though. It was surely better to learn that on the garage floor than out at sea. Later I replaced the boards with much stronger ones, and that was that. But I'd been shaken by the possibility you or the other boys could have been hurt. The worst damage came from my anger, when I went out afterward to buy a case of beer for your alcoholic friend. It was cynical, and I'm ashamed of it.

What I want to say now, though, without asking forgiveness, is that there was something else going on with me then. It wasn't ever you at all. It was just the rowdy situation, the edge, the knowing looks that The Guys were sending among themselves. I reacted as if I were the same age, an adolescent myself.

In fact, as soon as your friends arrived that day, all of you yelling and shoving each other and insulting each other in fun, I got a familiar feeling of dread. It's an irrational fear that first got into me when I was maybe fifteen. My parents had moved us down to Texas by then. The other boys in my new neighborhood had figured out that I was odd, and not just by being from the north. I'd made friends, you see, with a handsome and mysterious guy named Stephen, who didn't seem to mind that I was attracted to him, a guy so nonchalant about life that his indifference attracted me all the more. It was a crush, but the closest I had come to love. I remember he had perfectly smooth dark skin, white teeth, and hair so black and straight it was almost blue. Our school was thirteen miles away by yellow bus, so he and I had plenty of chance to get acquainted, but then he started driving to school on his own motorcycle and I missed him.

Every afternoon, as I watched longingly from the back seat out the rear window of our school bus, Stephen followed on his motorbike, swerving it recklessly when he saw me looking, and giving the finger to anyone else watching. He wore a brown leather jacket and jeans, he aced all his classes, and seemed not to remotely care about anything.

My longing grew until one afternoon, gazing in rapture as he drove behind the bus, I watched him straighten the motorcycle out, lock his handlebars by taking out the little handlebar key, and then clamp the key in his teeth as he slowly stood up on the seat of the roaring motorcycle, no hands, like a carnival stuntman, going fifty miles an hour on the Texas macadam. I was so in love.

How I ever got him off his bike and into the bus sitting next to me again is lost to memory, but it must have been like the gravity of the planets, it just happened, and not long after that we were spending the hot Texas summer riding together on his bike across the dried bed of White Rock Lake, entering a hidden path that took us back through the cottonwood trees, to the pond.

It was a sweet rotting place, a place that wasn't supposed to exist. I remember the smell of the big orange and blue crayfish we would catch, of the smoke of burning twigs as we cooked them on an inverted coffee can with beer-key holes around the top for the smoke; I remember the smell of Victor's skin and self, to me the smell of life. It was not acrid like the woman on the school bus I had tried to sit next to for appearances sake. His aura was sweet and compelling, and it stirred and provoked me in the most profound way. I guess you must have that sense around women.

One of the pleasures of reaching old age is to have an idea of what changes in a person and what doesn't, which is perhaps of particular interest to a gay man. We ask all the time: why am I this way? Is there some purpose in all this that I don't understand? It can be very liberating to be born different. It's a chance if not to attain wisdom, then at least to attain a point of view.

But at fifteen I didn't 'get' anything. At my school, queers were just people who wore green socks on Thursday, which I was careful not to do. In my high school there was a lot of glancing at ankles on Thursday mornings; in fact everybody seemed to spend a great deal of their time figuring out who was a queer and who wasn't. I considered myself to be unique but certainly not a queer, whatever that was. However with the advent of Stephen, the other kids decided for me. I hardly noticed that this had happened until a certain day that same summer.

As I mentioned, Stephen didn't care what other people thought. We wrestled a lot in the back yard, and not to win. He'd ride me around on that motorbike, and I'd be in heaven. The world seemed joyful. And one day, in that frame of mind, Stephen and I drove to the local swimming hole, a chain-link fenced off pond, really, with a sleepy lifeguard. We recognized some classmates in the water, horsing around, and decided it would be a good idea to go in. We left our pants, shirts and shoes at the edge. But as soon as we entered the water in our shorts, all the happy horseplay suddenly stopped, as if we had cholera. It was odd. I didn't get it.

We swam out, smiling, to where the other boys were. The water was deep. The older boys, who had stopped shouting at each other, kept treading water, slowly forming themselves into a slightly menacing circle around us, silent. I guess they had wordlessly decided to deal with us right there, first by splashing at us, as if in rowdy play, but ultimately by holding us under the water with their feet. At first it seemed like they were inviting us into the pack, but then, unable to surface, I realized they had other intentions.

I can never forget that sense of panic when I realized I was not going to come up. If I squirmed out from under the feet of one, there were other feet there to push me deeper. Just as I finally started inhaling water, coming in my nose, choking me through my mouth, my throat, a lifeguard intervened. Stephen, his face looking a little grey, had fought his way free, too, and we swam to shore, exhausted.

Stephen seemed to brush off the whole experience, but it took a while before I'd set foot out of the house again. When I did venture out, if I saw one of the swimming-hole bullies in his street clothes, he'd simply look away, not in shame, but in shunning. I was now beneath acknowledgment of any kind. And I still didn't know why.

Toward the end of summer, I felt like I had to take a walk back to the swimming place. There I was startled and frightened to spot one of the ringleaders inside the chain link enclosure, alone. He tried a little too hard not to notice me, walking around inside the fenced area as if casually looking for something. At first I didn't fully realize who he was because I kept looking at his near-naked body, his movements so unselfconscious. But then he suddenly turned and I saw his face, and his leering interest, or even desire, and at that moment I didn't even care that he'd been the instigator. Alone, he had eyes like an evil angel.

It was late afternoon and the boy kept coming closer. Finally he walked right over to where I was, and reached up and put his fingers through the chain link fence that separated us. "You should come in," he said, hanging there by his fingers, eye to eye. "Come on." I just looked him up and down. "Not today," I said, "I'll just watch."

He tried once more, then shrugged and went back and did some poses and dives and pretended to ignore me again, but I kept watching him, lost in the moment until he jumped in and started swimming toward me under water, or appeared to be, but his movements got slower and slower, as though he were falling asleep. With my eyes fixed on him, I reached up and clasped as he had my side of the fence that still separated us, staring, fascinated at his ability to stay under water.

He drifted down into the deep and dirty water, and then he laid spread out on the bottom. He had ceased moving and still I watched, certain that he was trying to fool me.

Then I heard a panicked shout from someone, and the lifeguard blasted his whistle, screaming for everyone get out of the water. The lifeguard plunged in and thrashed downward in the deep water, got hold of the boy's hair and brought him up.

I stayed where I was, to watch. Others crowded in front, but still I saw that the boy's face was blue. Vomit and mucous streamed out from his nose and mouth. The shaken lifeguard applied resuscitation to his back, squeezing the vomit out of his lungs through his nose and mouth.

Now, fifty years later, I remember in dreams every detail of the drowning, the failed resuscitation, the stretcher carrying his cold blueish body out through the chain-link gate to his waiting mother. And whenever I think of that, I wake up and my memory rewinds a little further, and I feel the cuts and scratches from his toenails on my shoulders, and I wonder why those had to be the only scars I'd ever bear out of my sudden love for him.

So maybe you can see, son, that when your friends got a little rowdy at the boat-turning, I felt the phantom scratches again on my shoulders. Maybe my boyhood scare explains why I built the boat at all... a way of never drowning. That idea is complicated, though, by what really happened to the kid at the swimming hole. The fact is, he was not carried out. He came to, he revived, he lived. And most of all, I tend to forget that the person who screamed for the lifeguard was me.

# The Things You'll Never Need

Stephen eventually did come driving past our house again. We resumed our wrestling and our motorcycle rides across the Texas lands, but our joy was gone, our innocence was dead from what had happened at the swimming place. Our last meeting occurred in my back yard, one day when we were tangled up in each other upon the thick prickly sod of St. Augustine grass, oblivious to the world, when I heard the glass patio door rumble open and my mother's choked voice call "John. Get in here." I slowly got up and went to the door.

"What?" I asked.

"You know what," she said, staring at me, utterly enraged. And she was right, I did know.

I heard Stephen quietly raising the kickstand on his motorbike and stomp-starting the motor. By the time I glanced back behind me, he was already out of sight. I'd have ridden off with him forever rather than go back into my mother's stale house. She might have wished for the same thing, rather than see my childhood end, and from then on she ceased to speak to me when we were alone, a circumstance she tried to avoid. If I went into a room, she went out.

I know it's too much to ask of you, son, to see that these events from long ago are still operational with me in situations that once might have spelled danger. But please believe me: It was never about you. I trust you more than anyone.

After what happened in the shed, I know you'll never set foot on this boat we built. You are as stubborn as I am. So for now the Ramona will stay docked in the Hudson River while I take a plane to the Orinoco. You wanted the boat built properly, so you said 'Why can't you do anything the right way?" and I just heard that as "Why don't you do things the way straight men do them?" That's unfair of me, but if anybody else asked me the same question, my answer would be "because I'm gay."  It's the same answer I give to myself when anyone is being mean to me without any apparent cause. If I find myself asking "why the hell are they treating me like that when I've done nothing wrong?" the explanation always turns out to be "because you're gay, stupid."

You know, when my own Grandpa Jan died he left me his woodworking tools – hand planes, wooden screw clamps, carving tools which I kept in a trunk in our garage. So that's where I went for a hammer to help a friend repair a cabinet. This was in Texas, after my mom had confirmed I was gay and

46

had stopped speaking to me. I was spending most of my time away from home. But when I came home to look for my hammer I found the tool trunk empty.

"Where are my tools?" I asked my mom.

"Oh those?" she said. "I sold them at a yard sale the other day." There was a knowing pause: "You won't ever be needing things like that."

# Freighter To Tangier

Okay, the plane has taken off and we are out over the Atlantic. I want to try to get to your question about my relations with women. I know it's important for you to know, but I don't want to go into my adolescent humiliations and college years right now, nor even my heiress stories. I think the first honest friendship I ever had with a woman was with Darleen. I'm not sure I ever told you about her, so here it is, short and sweet.

About ten years after I left my parents' home and finally landed in New York, it was Darleen the Monkey Woman who started teaching me about life from a poet's point of view. Like many of the other poets I hung out with then, I guess you'd say she was sort of a beatnik, saying "like, maaan, ..." and "cool." She worked days as a business stenographer and lived very frugally in a $40 flat on the Lower East Side, a block from the old Fillmore Auditorium  (before the music revolution.)

Whenever she had saved up a pile of money, from her job or else from selling pot, Marlene would book a freighter from New York to Tangier. She was afraid of flying, and there wasn't a plane going directly there at any rate. The ship was where I met her.

The crossing from Brooklyn to Africa usually took ten days unless there were storms and you had to put in at Portugal. If you were going the other direction, back to New York, you might have to wallow around helpless in mid-ocean if there was a storm and even then end up in Portugal. It was slow.

The power of an Atlantic storm may be the most awesome thing one could see ... to step out onto the slippery deck of that ship and be pickled with the spray from the almost warm wind as waves rise fifty feet above you, then to feel your entire ship be lifted above everything so you can see grey chaos to the horizon in all directions... huge waves like marching mountains, endless, what an incredible experience just to stay afloat in such conditions.

Many on the ship would get sick and stay in their cabins except for tea, but Darleen and I were thrilled. We sat in the lounge looking aft long into the night, watching the moon make crazy circles over the wake behind us, discussing Tangier.

All the old homo writers like Burroughs and Bowles and Genet used to live there or go there, and people like Darleen and I, who wanted to be writers but didn't write, swarmed around them like little sycophants. Darleen could tell you every Burroughs sighting, who was where, what was said, because she kept records. She wanted to categorize all her life on index cards, which she cross-referenced and kept in a kitchen closet in her apartment in New York. If you mentioned Sartre in a conversation, she might record what you said and file it with other remarks people had made about French philosophers. On the other hand, if you said it on Memorial Day, it might go into that file.

Although the hopelessness of this ordering of life never impinged on Darleen's determination, it did give someone like myself a lesson in how not to try to order experience. I think Darleen was a harbinger of the coming computer age in her own effort to digitize and make hierarchies of everything in life. It ruined life for her, just as computers have pretty much ruined life for the rest of us. But she carried on.

My Tangier file is full of names, but only my own memory tells me about an anonymous boy in Socco Chico who tried to steal my whole pack of cigarettes in a single grab and failed; he couldn't even steal my Gitanes. And where do you file mint tea? Under Jean Genet, a gay French writer who I sat beside at Cafe de Paris while waiting for a guy I'd met on the beach the day before, who took me (the boy, not Genet) to see Djilalla trance dancers and gave me hashish and other things. He carried his hash in the hood of his djellaba robe, and the two-part pipe in his sock. Most Tangerine harbor youth didn't seem to wear socks except for this purpose, just slipper-shaped Sbats, named for the Spanish word for shoe, Zapato.  File under Z.

When she was back in New York for her Summer Season, Darleen ran an experimental free school or atelier where people could offer to teach what they knew, and learn what they wanted from others. Darleen's contribution was to pose nude for Life Drawing.

For me, this was no particular treat. She didn't remove her monkey-like wig, which made her naked postures even more bizarre, however a plumber named Barney Lipperman came to every class. He was a dumpy man in his late fifties who'd been unlucky in love. He had lived with his mother all his life in a nearby building that he owned, on the Lower East Side.

The fact that Barney owned a building was not lost on Darleen, who needed locations in which to create her ateliers. She also needed plenty of closets for file cards. So Barney was encouraged to come to Life Drawing, where he scrawled stick figures and studied the naked model carefully.

Yes, after Barney's mother died Darleen ended up with the building, where she installed theatrical lights in the living room so different moods or topics in her conversations could be accompanied by aptly colored lighting.

By that time she also worked nights as an on-call Kelly Girl, using her added income to buy musical instruments, which she stored in her home as well. Eventually she had a Les Paul guitar, a bass guitar, an amplifier for vocals, and a drum set with four cymbals. She didn't know how to play any of the instruments, nor would she allow them to be touched by anyone who did.

After over a year's deliberation she realized that hers would probably be a solo career, so she stopped referring to "the band" and chose guitar, which she played not at all, and a week later booked herself into a bar. A lot of us went. She made it through one of her compositions, called "Where Am I?" which I believe was the only lyric also.

She didn't make it all the way through the next song, though. The audience got serious with their complaints and she insulted them back and got kicked out. After that debacle she sold me her drums, which I later played when I joined an all-psychiatrist band, the Nocturnal Emissions, an equally unmusical group started years afterward by your godfather Andrew. Our debut met with a reception similar to that of Darleen.

Just so you know, Darleen never actually married Barney, but she still inherited the building when he died. At that time she owned a small house in Tangier, an apartment building in New York, a lake in Maine with six cabins on it, and a three-cylinder car she called Little Polluter, all acquired through the salary of a temporary secretary with a monkey wig. I'm sure about the real estate holdings because she repeated the list to me in a phone conversation many years later when she called after having had a vision that told her I was dead. This was before the internet, so how she got my unlisted number I don't know, unless the vision gave her that also; and why she called a dead man I don't know either, unless in hopes of getting her drum set back, which wasn't going to happen.

We are high above the Atlantic now, and I see freighters far below, tiny dots crawling toward Tangier. I think about Eddie with the Ice Cream Pants, who I met in front of the old Fillmore East one morning and took home to Darleen's while we waited for her to come back from Tangiers.

Eddie who stayed – what a stunner he was – and how he could survive on his wits. All he had in the world were a pair of very shiny shoes with two colors of maroon leather, no socks, a string around his neck, and his pair of ice cream colored pants. Bare chest, never a shirt. Pants and shoes was all he needed.

How many Eddies have I known? Firehouse Eddie, dressed like the Philip Morris bellhop, a callboy of the first order, with stripes down the side of his pants. At the first Firehouse Dance in New York, he picked me up by casually picking up my beer and drinking it while looking elsewhere, pretending not to notice me. Please.

Now the clouds below us grow dark and look like mountains, jungles, intimations of the Orinoco, of the Andes. Far off on the horizon are bands of red – orange – pale white and then sudden blue. A single flashing red light moves in the sky parallel with us. Where is it going? To Venezuela, like me? To the Orinoco Delta? Or will they descend to the halfway islands? Are we over Virgin Gorda? That's a landmark for me…okay, that's a story, too. Here you go.

# The Treasure King

In a café of red painted boards, sipping a cup of
Nescafe with evaporated milk, we try to decide where we are.
A map is rolled out on the oilcloth table top. An accordion is
playing "Jesus loves me" across the street. Rain taps on the
roof, or maybe it's just the rattling palms.   Back in let's say
1969, the year America  really changed, I was down in Tortola,
looking across the water toward the island of Virgin Gorda,
then a simple place, just jungle, green hills, two tiny hidden
villages at the ends of the island, empty beaches between. It
was an hour away, they said, by the old wooden boat that
daily crossed that patch of the blue Caribbean.

I had gone down to the islands in company with an
old doctor friend, Jean Cook, who'd been hired for the
summer to start a summer camp and school on behalf of some
radical Quakers for whom he and I had worked before, up in

Vermont. The owners had taken it into their heads to create an intercultural youth survival experience in what they thought would be paradise.

Dr. Cook , a gay African-American man, had spent time in the Caribbean, in Haiti. His enthusiasm for this new project in the British Virgins had been evident in his phone call to me, but I was reluctant to leave my job just to go down there for three months. But I was able to get a leave of absence at Time Magazine, where I reported for the New York Bureau.

Jean and I took a plane to San Juan and then to Tortola, and now we waited in the café for our meet-up with the third man, Bill Zeller, who'd been sent as Director of he project. We'd never met him, but we assumed that would be no problem. He arrived in khaki, stopping at the doorway, looking past us at first, then realizing we were the ones.

He introduced himself as an army survival specialist. Jean offered that he too had served, as a medic. In World War Two. 'Oh, so you're the *doctor*?" asked Zeller. This was going to be bad. I had to speak up. "And dean of a famous medical college." Zeller squinted. Jean was ready for a long summer.

We finished our coffee then left together to walk past clusters of one room houses on the hillside, "reminiscent of Africa," Jean said. We followed the dirt path down to the harbor, where the local boat, the Typhon, was waiting for its daily run to Virgin Gorda. Our used khaki tents, donated by the British Army station, had been delivered and left there, dockside, along with boxes of supplies ordered by Zeller, which were being loaded on board.

Typhon sat quietly on the morning water, grumbling out a cloud of blue smoke. Dr. Cook advised us to sit on top of the cabin with the livestock, explaining that the interior would be occupied strictly by women. I noticed that the searchlight atop the deckhouse was merely a can nailed to a cross of wood. Inside, the gas-engine sump pump bailed out a steady stream of water, its exhaust filling the cabin. The ladies disregarded this and merely sat there in the smoke with their umbrellas raised. Mr. Zeller made space for himself and sat there with them.

Typhon strains at her mooring ropes. Her thirty two feet of soggy rotting wood wants to be off. The captain, Mr. George, looses off the mooring, scampers inside and pushes the throttle forward. The engine belly growls. Typhon leans into the morning seas. Soon we see Virgin Gorda ahead, and a friendly soul points out our beach at Nale Bay, where someone has left, hauled up on the shore, a flat whaler-type boat with an outboard engine on it.

"I had it sent up," yelled Zeller. "It's ours for the summer." We slowed toward shore. From the idling Typhon Zeller dived in and swam to the beach, then cranked up the Whaler and brought it back out, impressing us with his ability in two trips to unload our supplies onto the beach, and then one more to bring me and Jean and duffel. We were there.

Oh at first our camping site seemed paradisiacal – from the beach we could watch faraway pelicans gliding in formation toward the Dog Islands, banking over the stirring water then plunging one at a time into the bay. Under our own feet waves lapped and hissed into the sand. … Behind us palm trees marched up the steep hillsides, raising their rattling fronds in the wind, as if alarmed. As soon as we came ashore we spotted a shady apple tree at the jungle margin of the beach. There, under the tree, we set our provisions and cleared off a place to sleep that night.

The Typhon had soon gone off again, around the point that defined our bay, and then we could no longer hear her engine, and all was silent. There was no other noise.

Jean sat in the shade of the apple tree, taking photographs all round. Zeller stood next to him, gazing around in a proprietory manner. Rather than try to make conversation I went off alone, leaving them under the tree to work out their dominance problems.

There was no other person to be seen for miles, anywhere. There was no boat on the horizon, no dwelling within view, ashore or across the sea. Stepping inland, hiking into the scrub vegetation I soon stepped on a sharp spine, which left a wound in the sole of my foot that would remain unhealed for weeks. Behind the beautiful sand beach was only thick brush, thorns, cactus and mud, stinking mud redolent of disease. I came upon an old stone well back there, probably dug in the days when this had been part of a British plantation, but now the well was just filled with scum. Huge obscene land crabs all around scuttled and clicked away at my approach. I turned back, concealing my discouragement.

But the beach of Nale Bay, our salvation, was right there, still calm, still that beautiful blue-green color except for the brown patches further out that showed where the coral reef hid just below the surface. We sat quiet and tired until evening. Faraway columns of showers marched across the horizon toward the Dog Islands. The two older men had spread out their sleeping bags under the apple tree, so I reluctantly did likewise. Later that night we learned about sand fleas.

In the morning, Zeller's nose sported an unflattering sunburn from the previous day. We just lay still, watching him. Lacking anything to eat because he had forgotten a can opener, he ate one of the apples from overhead, disliking it. But he was in charge, an army vet, and he made clear that he would be first in everything. He ate the apple and another in spite of its taste. "Local wild food," he explained. We declined.

About an hour later Zeller's mouth was swollen and he couldn't swallow at all. Though Jean was a doctor, he had never seen this, so we talked Zeller into the Whaler boat to bring him to the British doctor in the village at the other end of the island. As we climbed aboard, Zeller pointed back in alarm to the line of trees above the beach. There, out of the wall of vegetation, stepped a tall, very ancient man wearing a wide-brim straw hat with an orange band, and a tropical shirt and green khaki pants. He was waving a machete in greeting. This was Waldemore Creque, (Creaky,) who I'd later learn was the oldest man on the island. His companion, who stepped out behind him, was an even taller man with wens on his face. I recognized him as Alonzo George, the captain of the Typhon.

Creque called out to us in his heavy island patois, pointing to the apple tree as I stepped back out of the boat and went to greet them. I told him we were just about to leave for the doctor, and why. "Then he did eat the manchineal?" he asked? I said "Yes."

Creque looked alarmed. "Them is the apple of Adam and Eve!" he cried. "Them apple is bad poison!"

'Oh yes." Said Mr. George, nodding vigorously as if speaking to someone else on the other side of him, who he could see but we could not. "Oh yes, um hummm." Dr. Cook left Zeller in the boat and also came up to greet both men with a deferential handshake. I noticed Mr. Creque had few teeth, and his pants were ripped, but he seemed the most dignified person I had ever met in my young life.

Creque continued to shout. I would come to learn that he always shouted. Being new to the islands I could hardly understand his accent, but I got the meaning: "Don't even sleep under that tree," he was saying. "If the rain does come, the drops off that tree will eat your skin."

"Yes, yes," Mr. George agreed, nodding to his invisible companion. "It's true."

Zeller was revving the engine on the boat, so we told the visitors we would be back later and hoped they would come again so we could have a longer talk. Once we reboarded, before we sat, Zelle revved the boat backward into the bay, like a bad parent trying to threaten kids to hurry up.

Of course, Zeller was the one who was suffering, so he did have a claim to urgency. Once we got to the village, the English doctor looked him over, said yes it was manchineal, foolish to touch it let alone eat it. A few days and it would subside, he said, turning back to talk shop with Dr. Cook. I thought Zeller was more uncomfortable with the fraternity of the doctors than he was with his own mouth burns. He paced. He wanted to go back. That was fine with me, too. Medical news was boring and I couldn't wait to go find Mr. Creque.

When the old island man and I did meet again, we became immediate friends, and before long he was my guide and teacher, in island life and more. We spent every day together talking about the plants, the history, the weather. He showed me how to make fish traps from branches of the loblolly tree, showed me where to pick limes, where and how to plant Tanias. And meanwhile we built up the encampment, to receive the twenty-some young adventurers who would soon come from the U.S. Hopefully we would be hosting some island kids as well, but none of the local parents seemed ready to consent to such an experiment.

After almost a month of preparations, there was still nothing that looked like a school, and we three northern men were already exhausted. The encampment had only a crude kitchen hacked out of the underbrush, a pit privy, and the horribly ragged, hot tents given us by the British Army on

Tortola. It looked like an abandoned Japanese WWII outpost, with flies.

Our food consisted primarily of five gallon plastic buckets of USDA Surplus Pork Tails and Pork Snouts, for which we paid incredible amounts in the village's only store. The bay, we learned by snorkeling, was full of Moray eels, barracuda, poisonous sea urchins, and other ocean fauna including large sharks that came in to feed on the reef fish at dusk. Just the place for kids, I thought.

To me, there was a sense of danger, of doom over the whole enterprise, but every morning Mr. Waldemore Creque and Mr. Alonzo George would appear with big smiles, bright clothes and sharp machetes to teach us something new and lighten my spirits.

One morning they arrived by sea, rowing around the point of land that created our bay. We heard the oars creaking before we saw their old blue wooden boat piled high with nets. Creque, it turned out, had discerned from the color of the water the day before that there would be a school of tasty fish called Karans passing that way soon.

He and Mr. George stopped rowing and sat silent in the bay, for a very long while it seemed to me, until suddenly they erupted into shouting and throwing of nets and rowing and hauling and more shouting as they pulled in their nets. We could see they were filling the boat with flipping silver fish. Then, paying no attention to us, they piled the nets up astern and headed their skiff toward the distant village, Mr. George rowing like mad and Mr. Creque standing in the stern, yelling and blowing on a conch-shell trumpet to alert everyone down-island that they had a catch and were coming in to sell fresh fish.

The use of the conch as a trumpet, we later learned from Mr. Creque, came from slave days, when it was used to communicate in the war against the British. When the colonizers heard the conches sounding all over Virgin Gorda and Tortola, they knew their time was up, so they took with them what they could, but buried the coin and bullion that was too heavy. They planned to come back to retrieve their gold when they had more British guns. But most never did come back, he said, so Virgin Gorda became known by rumor as the Treasure Island.

Mr. Creque willingly shared all his lore with the children once they arrived. Dr. Cook and I sat back and listened too. We were feeling more comfortable about the whole enterprise by then, since the one thing we did know how to do was educate kids. With the constant waves and breeze it all felt settled to us.

Then, one night at a beach campfire, Creque told the kids about Sprauve the Treasure King, who years before had actually found four gold pieces right there on the beaches of Nale Bay. But the spirit of the person who had buried it came back to bother Sprauve, he said. In the kitchen where the treasure hunter usually worked down in the village, hot grease spilled on him and burned his hands and face, torturing his features beyond recognition. The next year his wife was mysteriously killed, shot in their own house, and so finally Sprauve realized they were cursed, and went back to Nale Bay to throw the coins back to the water where he found them. And nobody, said Creque, nobody had dug there since. There's still plenty treasure in Long Bay, he warned, so don't you boys ever touch it.

Dr. Cook and I took him as seriously as the kids did, but of course I'm sure you already know that Mr. Zeller smirked about it and later decided to make it into a game. He announced they would all go treasure hunting.

Mr. Creque saw them out there at low tide next day, digging. He and Mr. George didn't display anger, but turned their backs, left the bay, through the briars up the hill toward The Bond where they lived, and next day they didn't return.

And I have to tell you what you also already know, that from then on our grand experiment at Nale Bay began to come apart. Like Sprauve the Treasure King, we were to get three warnings. And this was how it went:

The evening after Mr. Zeller started the kids digging in the coral sand, one of the treasure hunters, a boy of about twelve, hid near the beach instead of going to his tent. He was always the most frightened and lonely of the bunch. Dr. Cook sometimes had to console him like a five year old. The night after the so-called treasure hunt, this little fellow, alone and sad, inexplicably put on his mask and snorkel and swam out toward the reef all alone at dusk. I realized it only because I saw the red tip of his snorkel moving through the water far out over the reef. Then at the same time I saw the fin of a shark nearby. In panic I ran down the beach and pushed our boat into the water, but by the time I got the engine to catch, the boy had already started swimming to shore with the shark fin close behind but then veering away. The child never knew it had been there.

After the shaking kid was tucked in that night and all the rest were asleep, I went back out to think on the beach. I sat looking at the wondrous Southern constellations, the few star-bright clouds over the Caribbean. From a nearby ledge of coral, exposed at low tide, I heard a slurping sound. I was jumpy anyway; the suddenness of it startled me, so I crept up on the noise. Was it a joke? The camp was asleep.

Once I got close enough I had to smile at myself. It was just our big cast iron Dutch oven pot that one of the dishwashers had left inverted on the coral shelf. The sound came from the waves sucking out from under it as the tide went out. I retrieved the pot and returned it to its hook in the kitchen, then hurried a little more than necessary to my sleeping bag in the army tent.

The second warning came in a very different way the next day. Dr. Cook stayed with the boys so I could take the Whaler back to the port village to get some more pig snouts and Long Life milk. Zeller went too, because he had also arranged to buy a flat of imported cabbage plants to start his own garden at Long Bay, independent of Mr. Creque who had planted local crops for us. He didn't trust me with the plants.

The day was bright, and with a strong breeze behind us we got to the village bay, reached the pass through the coral quickly, and docked. Zeller and I by then hardly spoke to one another. In town, he did the ordering and buying, and kept his accounts, while I did some visiting. Once Zeller had his cabbage plants he wanted to return to camp at once.

Loaded with all our supplies, the Whaler was up to her gunnels, up to the rim. Though I was anxious to get back, I was worried about the overloading. Zeller was not. He jumped in the boat, placed his briefcase with all the camp's money and documents on top of the parcels, alongside the cabbage plants, then he yanked the cord and started the motor.

His face was so very sunburned, I remember, and he was beginning to wear an expression of permanent contempt and impatience. I got in the boat, but before I was even seated he gave it full throttle against the harbor rules, and thrashed through the channel, out into the open water of the Caribbean.

Naturally it was a very rough day. The morning ride downwind had been exhilarating with only mists of spray in our face and the motor humming. We had seen a huge sting ray leap full out of the water at a place called Cow Mouth, and we had seen sharks there, all of them eating something, thrashing the water. Now, on the return trip, with motor straining, we drove against the wind and waves. The Whaler wallowed, and as we reached Cow Mouth the bow dipped under a wave. Just like that we took on water. We swamped.

Now Whalers are unsinkable, made with closed-cell foam, but this was a loaded Whaler. The boat settled just barely under water, with the top of the outboard engine still above the water and still running. I jumped out into the water to lighten the load so we could bail, figuring Zeller would do the same, but he seemed paralyzed, hesitating. Then, leaving the briefcase with all the money and documents behind, he grabbed the cabbage plants, held them over his head, and jumped overboard too. He must have seen Mutiny on the Bounty. Eerily, the boat continued to travel slowly ahead on its own as I swam toward shore, thinking of the sharks. When I looked back I saw the whaler was now turning itself, as if steered, into a circle, the running motor's top still held above water by the boat's flotation. As I watched, it came right for Zeller, the prop passing his neck only by grace.

I reached shore first, clothes heavy, feeling exhausted, unable to do more than watch Zeller thrash as he tried unsuccessfully to get the plants to safety. The Whaler itself came around again, and sputtered toward the rocks, until finally its engine stopped just short of the boat crashing. I hastened to it as best I could, lest the waves beat it to pieces on the rocks. But the boat waited there placidly, deliberately, up to her gunnels. The briefcase with all our documents, money, kids passports, everything was soaked in sea-water. The cans of food were soon to be without labels so we'd be having to eat by surprise. Zeller's garden was now cabbage of the sea.

That night I had to really think over whether I should continue with this unsafe adventure with other people's kids.

Dr. Cook was going to return to the states, his agreed formal responsibilities now over. He had to go back to teach at the medical school. The boys, twenty of them, sensing my state of mind, sent a delegation asking me to stay. But I finally decided my resignation would force the owners back in the states to some kind of conclusion. Hurricane season was coming.

Then came the third warning. That night I checked each tent to spend some time with the young people under my care and to try to explain myself. I promised I wouldn't leave until someone else came. Once I knew the kids were asleep, I checked each tent again, then walked the perimeter of the camp, stopping at the kitchen to make sure the Dutch oven was on its hook. Then I went out to my spot on the beach under a full moon and tried to rethink my decision. A few minutes went by. Then, directly in front on me, on the coral ledge, there suddenly began a familiar slurping sound. It was, I could see in the moonlight, the inverted Dutch oven. We only had one.

This time I left it there, ran back to the tent, tied the door flaps together inside, and lowered the mosquito netting. Like a child myself, I pulled my head in with the rest of me, curling up inside my sleeping bag. It was a hot, bright, sleepless night of course. After about an hour, an army of huge hollow-sounding land crabs circled the tent. They were foul-smelling, noisy clacking things. As the night went on they dug their way under and came into the tent, each crab about the size of a saucepan and weighing five pounds or so. With their pincers they climbed up the inside of the fabric, then pinced their way up toward the peak of the tent, dangling like aerialists over us. And then one by one they let go and fell on our heads. Boys screamed, I didn't know what was happening, but I was angry enough to start kicking the crabs out the tent opening.

The night passed with me standing guard over the sleepless youngsters and ejecting any land crabs that arrived late. Before dawn I was on my way up through the brush to the top of the island where I knew Mr. Creque lived. Little harmless hermit crabs scuttled ahead of me in the dust.

It took something like half an hour to reach The Bond, the settlement at the top of the island. Creque greeted me joyfully, sat me down in his cool breezy house with its cement floor to eat scrambled eggs from his chickens and soda crackers from a tin. and to have fresh water from the rain cistern. Mr. George joined us, and I brought up the problem. "There is a lot of trouble in the camp."

"Yes, yes," said Creque, and he and Mr. George started yelling in island talk which translated said we tried to tell you, we tried to say don't mess around with spirits. They said they'd warned me that that class of things would 'mash me up good.'

Creque sat down beside me. "Last night," he said, "as I slept I had a vision of a woman. She came up and said Wally take me home."

"Oh yes," yelled Mr. George.

Creque said he told the woman that he knew she was nothing but a spirit, and as soon as he said so, she vanished.

I asked Mr Creque if he had power over spirits, and he said only God had that class of power. I asked if the kids were in danger, if the kid with the snorkel was marked. And the best I can do to transcribe what he actually said was 'Them spirit just play with he, but if he does dig in Nale Bay one more time them spirit will kill he." I believed him entirely, and he knew it.

Together we walked down from the Bond on his trail, the two of them yelling back and forth all the while. Mr. Creque carried with him a small bottle of fluid and a Bible.

At Nale Bay the boys were up early, trying to clear land for Bob's still-promised one-day cabbage garden. The kids looked so ragged and sad, still like Lord of the Flies, scratching the ground with hoes , while the red-faced Zeller stood at the side like a Southern sheriff, watching warily.

We passed them quietly and went on to the beach. At the water margin Mr Creque said some words. He poured the liquid, told me the spirits had been sent back, and that now he and Mr. George would show these boys how to really make a garden.

"That's right," said Mr. George,"

"Cassavas! Limes and squash!"

"Oh yes!!" And ignoring Mr. Zeller they unsheathed their machetes and stepped alongside the boys to work.

Those twenty boys all survived the summer, because the people they needed to watch out for them were Creque and George, the island men who actually knew something.

Many years later, after I had gone back to the life of a New York journalist, I reached a point in life when I was increasingly troubled in spirit, closing in on despair, so one grim day I decided to write a letter to the wisest man I knew, addressing it to Mr. Waldemore Creque, The Bond, Virgin Gorda, BVI. At that time he was over ninety years old. He had thirty-five great grandchildren. I felt he knew more about life than anyone else I'd ever met.

A month later, in a clear beautiful hand came his reply. John he said the Lord is bringing you back to us. And here is the plan and it is a good plan. You grow a garden. Grow limes, mango, and cassava. Then you will be happy. Come and see me before I die. And that will be a good plan. Waldemore Creque.

I did exactly as he said, and yes, it was a good plan. You can always figure out a way to grow a garden wherever you are, and as you know, son, I have always done so since. And I did go to visit him, just before the island was going to be developed for tourists, which thankfully he did not live to see.

One night he and I looked up in the night sky and we saw a satellite moving rapidly eastward. When he asked what I thought about it I told him how it got there, rockets and so forth. Had I seen it go up with my own eyes, he asked? No. He looked across Drake's Passage with his own ancient eyes, and with an arm on my shoulder said, "Don't trouble yourself with that class of things." So I didn't, and I don't.

And now I am flying over the islands, where Mr. Creque lies buried, and I'm glad he doesn't have to look at the winking lights on our wingtips as the plane hurtles through the night toward the Orinoco Delta, and the coast of another continent.

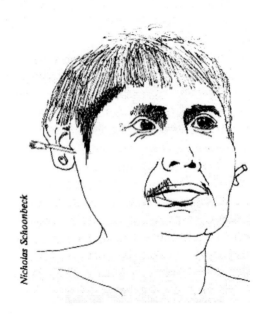

Nicholas Schoonbeck

# A Bridge To The Warrao

Sometime in prehistory, an indigenous people called Warao
fled their marauding neighbors, the Caribs and Arawaks, and
adapted to a life in stilt houses standing above the vast, hostile
delta of Venezuela's Orinoco River. Here, some 15,000 Warao
still live peaceably, eating fish and grubs and cakes made from
Moriche palms. Their houses are connected to one another by
wooden log bridges, which are built and repaired as

community projects, under leadership of the shaman, who is also the civic leader. In April of 1988 I found myself in a propeller plane, flying over such a village in the labyrinthine delta, en route to a landing strip at Tucupita, a trading center for the Orinoco basin.

My friend Charles Briggs, a Vassar anthropologist, had recently returned from a year's fieldwork in the Delta, and had told me the government was trying to make inroads into Warao culture by promising newer and better bridges for the villages.

Naturally, Charles said, this would result in the loss of the community-making ritual of the bridge-making, but beyond that, after some villages had agreed and had taken down the old bridges, the government had failed to put in new ones, thus leaving the stilt houses in splendid isolation, a first step toward exploitation by the outside world.

Upon hearing Charles's story, I spoke immediately with other Friends on our yearly meeting's Right Sharing Committee, who agreed to send $800 to the Warao so they could put their old bridges back. The money would be used for gasoline for outboards and food for families whose bread-finders would not be hunting and gathering while they rebuilt the infrastructure of the villages.

The problem was how to get the money to the Warao. The most practical method, since we knew of no Quakers in that area, was to send the money through the Capuchin monks who had lived in the area for some time.

Charles called the bishop, explaining that the money was available but could only be spent on self-renewing projects, which would be administered by the people themselves. An inquiry carne back; could some of the money be used to repair a chapel, which was also used for a community meeting hall? I said no. The question had aroused my worst fears: that instead of helping the Warao protect their own culture we would serve those who sought to feed on it. Nevertheless, I carried the $800 check down to the Venezuelan bank in New York, and it was telexed to Tucupita.

Two months later, I was preparing to visit friends in Caracas, and hoping to make a side trip to the Orinoco to see how the bridges were coming. But on the day before my departure, Charles called, saying the bishop was claiming the money had never arrived. That was disheartening, but I was determined to follow it through, stopping again at the bank in New York for evidence of the transaction before going on to Caracas and doing the same thing there. Yes, the money had gone to Caracas, they said, and it was in the bank at Tucupita.

Now I was in a quandary. What was the point of going there if the bishop had spent our money on his chapel and was going to claim it had never arrived? My Spanish was so poor I wouldn't be able to do any delicate negotiations. My friends in Caracas sat me down and said, "Just go there." So I went. Now I was looking out the window of this old plane, wondering whether it would even be able to land at the airstrip. We bounced on one wheel halfway down the runway, nearly piling into the trees before stopping. Then a taxi with crosses hanging from its rear-view mirror took me to the bishop's palace, a rundown edifice in a rundown river town. Even at nine in the morning, the humidity and heat were transporting.

The Apostolic Vicar of Christ wasn't in, so I left my card, and went instead to the bank. On the way, I locked eyes with two older Warao men, finding immediate recognition. It took the officer of the bank less than a minute to locate the money transfer. "It has been here since February," she said. I added that to my other evidential papers, and marched back to the bishop's palace, where he had now arrived.

He was a sallow, long-faced fellow with eczema; he looked like the head psychologist at a mental hospital. When asked, he refused to acknowledge the money until I produced the papers. "Still," he said, "I haven't received official notification." A weak explanation, I thought. Then he said the government had begun to repair the bridges anyway because it was an election year. Maybe he could think of something to use the money for next year. At this point my limited Spanish failed me. He must have used our money to buy new costumes for his priests, or maybe to erect a big idol of Jesus or a cross in the jungle. Still – I checked myself. There was something missing-a failed connection.

We agreed to meet again at two, with an interpreter. I sat in the park for an hour, having silent meeting with the sloths in the trees overhead. The sloth, with its perpetual smile and deliberate manner, would be the Quaker of animals, I decided. It was difficult for me to center down; I kept imagining the jungle being ennobled by the erection of a lurid cross, for people who needed something literally concrete to worship.

Some kids pulled a sloth out of a tree by the back of its neck and tried to make it drink what looked like wine. Sloths can move when circumstances require, and it thrashed to be released. At the river shore, drunken Warao could barely stay in their dugouts. All of them wore clothes, and some of them wore crosses.

A leading began to get hold of my mind, and by two o'clock it was getting clearer, as though purified by the heat. With the bishop again, I asked if he knew about Quakers. He said he had read about us in school, but had no special knowledge. I explained our belief that the Inner Light in everyone was the manifestation of Holy Spirit that Jesus said God would send as the Comforter; I explained our testimonies of simplicity and peace, and I explained that we didn't proselytize. In fact, I said, we made it difficult for people to become Quakers . . . it took a long time. He looked at me with more recognition and tentative acceptance. "We have trouble with evangelists here," he finally declared. "They come and confuse the people and then leave. We Capuchins are here to serve the indigenous people. If they choose to come to the mission and learn Christianity, that's their business. We hope they will, but only if they are ready." Each of us had worried the other was an evangelist.

"Most Quakers believe the same way you do," I said. "The evangelists could stay home."

"They come here in buses, with loud speakers," he said. There was still a vast difference between us, but at least one difference had been bridged. We kept on, speaking in a general way as he continued to guess what I wanted. After another half-hour's discussion he finally said, "There is one place called Joruba de Guayo where there are no bridges, and the government won't be going there because it isn't visible. They also have no school. Suppose we used this money to build the bridges and to make a school?"

"Who'd be the teacher? A nun?"

"This is strictly a civic project, not Catholic." He seemed injured that I still mistrusted him.

"I wouldn't even care if it was a nun if she was a good teacher," I said. And then, finally, I asked him about the Warao's success at remaining a peaceable people while the tribes around them lived upon warfare, wife-beating, and male hierarchies, just like at home. "The Warao have nothing to disturb them," he said, "or they didn't until alcohol came along."

"Nothing disturbs the Yanomamo either," I said, "but they have axe fights every day." And probably they had problems with alcohol, too. Was it the alcohol that made them drunks? An old question surfaced . . . The philosopher Gregory Bateson said that there were two basic forms of life, the symmetrical, like a starfish, and the complementary, like the lobster. The patterns existed in relationships between people, too. Ice skating duets would be symmetrically related. Basketball players would be complementary. Bateson said symmetrical relationships could not survive in a complementary world. Two evenly matched boxers would fight until one won and one lost, achieving emphatic complementarity.

Alcoholics were people raised to be symmetrical, who could only participate in the complementary world by being drunk, even unconscious. Were the Warao a successfully symmetrical people who now had to deal with complementary cultures outside? Is that why the drunkenness occurred at the boundaries?

Their art designs were beautifully and totally symmetrical. And I had seen two adolescent boys in the park sitting unconcernedly with their hands in each other's laps. You'd never see such an unselfconscious symmetrical male relationship in our culture, I thought, least of all among priests. They lived in the most rigid male hierarchy on earth, beginning with God as a guy who lives in the sky, going down by increments to the monks in the delta who got their orders from the bishop by short wave radio.

Well, it was all a puzzlement, and even the boys of the morning in the park were more complicated than I would have liked them to be. They hadn't been giving the *paresa* – the sloth – any wine, they said, it was fruit juice. They loved their paresas. Would I like them to get one out of the tree for photos? No, I said, no posing necessary.

From the window of my room that night I saw a family of Warao people come in by dugout to buy some orange popsicles. Not so bad, I thought, we do have some worthwhile things to offer them. I spent the evening thinking about how this leading had brought me to such a place, and to such an encounter not with the Indians, but with a Catholic bishop. Perhaps our business was not finished.

What would it be like to teach in a stilt house in the delta? I wondered. Would my son back home like it? He was undoubtedly home watching television without me there to insist that he turn it off, while here in the Orinoco, drunken Warao fell out of their canoes. In the park, sloths smiled. In the palace, the bishop gathered up his robes and went upstairs to the radio transmitter, to tell the people in Joruba de Guayo that construction on the new bridges and school would begin the next day.

© 1988-1989 Friends Publishing Corp., All Rights Reserved

# Hearts
# of Palm

*A Story Retold by John Schoonbeck*

Despite the late hour, it was hot in the jungle, and the frogs were beginning to sing. The Vicar of Christ greeted the Indian leader, the Wiziratu, indicating that they should both sit on stumps of manaca palms. "Today," said the Vicar, "I will explain to you how the world began. But first I will listen to your own story."

The Wiziratu thought a moment, then sat forward and began a recitation. "There is a Roaster, " he began, "married to two sisters, with a son by the youngest sister. The wives cut Moriche palms and scoop out flour from the trunks; the Roaster and his son go into the jungle to hunt animals for roasting. "

"How old is this son?" asked the Vicar.

"He has been all different ages," said the Wiziratu. "One night that Roaster goes into the jungle and dies. At early dark the wives say 'where is our husband? He does not come back.' Then that man comes in with their son and roast meat 'Here, my wives,' he says. 'I am tired. Lay my son beside me and you two eat this roast meat.'

"Excuse me," said the Vicar, "I thought the man had died in the jungle." The Wiziratu indicated that this was so, as if the Vicar were finally beginning to understand. "When he is gone to sleep the wives look on top of the roast meat and they see something. They see their husband's penis. 'Look,' they say. 'That Roaster is not our husband! Our husband is dead, and now No-Indian is sleeping with our child. What shall we do?' "

The Vicar wiped his brow against the perpetual heat, wondering how the Roaster could roast himself. He wished the story didn't have to mention the word "penis." "Have we come to the end?" he inquired.

"No," said the Wiziratu, "Not til I say 'It is finished.' "

"This was supposed to be about creation, the beginning of everything. Will you mention other body parts?"

"No. Those wives took the child and ran off. When No-Indian woke up he chased them so they had to pull out their pubic hairs to make spears, thorns, and knives to throw in his path."

Silently the Vicar decided to endure these ideas, because he knew the old Indian was too ignorant to be modest. He allowed the old man to continue. "Soon they came to Frog, and went inside her house. Frog stood at the entrance. When No-Indian came she said, 'No women have come here,' and she killed him with a spear."

"But he was a spirit, wasn't he?" the sly Vicar reminded him. "You can't kill a spirit, can you?" The Wiziratu simply continued, as if he hadn't been interrupted. "His anus became the North Star. Frog sent the sisters out to pull manioc and she kept the child at home. When the sisters returned they said 'Now where is our child?' Frog says 'What child? This is my grandson.' So Haburi had three mothers."

"But only one actual mother," corrected the Vicar.

"No, I just told you he had three. Now the child Haburi went out to make a bongo boat. One sank, then another sank, then one floated and he paddled across the big water to Trinidad. Frog tried to follow him but he threw water in her mouth so she became a frog. Now she sits sadly in a tree and says, 'oowang, oowang, oowang.' Now it is finished."

"Ah," said the Vicar, unlacing his fingers and warming to the task ahead. "So your God is a Frog-woman."

"What do you mean your God?"

The Vicar smiled benignly. "I'll tell you the story about God," he said. "In the beginning was heaven and earth."

"What is heaven?"

"What is not the world," the Vicar found himself saying.

"Is it like this place here?"

"No, heaven is different from this world, it's where God lives. This is the earth."

"Like No-Indian, you mean, he lives here but he's not come from here." No point in arguing, so he continued with Genesis. "There was water all over the earth, and it was dark." His listener was impressed with the Vicar's knowledge on this point, since the great alluvial fan of the Orinoco Delta in Venezuela was almost all water. The Vicar said "God separated the light from the darkness, and he divided the waters and put heaven in between."

"Yes I thought so. Heaven is here, between the waters."

The Vicar was already becoming impatient with the interruptions. He felt he must get to the end if the Wiziratu was ever to learn the Truth. "Next God divided waters from land to make earth, and He made plants grow. Then He made the sun and moon."

"This story is very wise," the Wiziratu said. "God put the sun in the day where we could see it, and the moon in the night where it is supposed to be." For some reason this made the Vicar uncomfortable. Had he gotten the order wrong? Was there daylight before God put the sun up there? But he plunged ahead. "Finally God brought forth every living creature, and then made man and woman. And he saw that it was good." He slapped his thigh.

"Is that all?" asked the other man.

"Yes. That is how everything was made. Frogs were made on the fifth day, by God."

"All the frogs?" The Wiziratu knew this was not true, but the Vicar was his guest, so he changed the subject to make a compliment. "That man God is really a divider! He divides the water. He divides the world. Does he divide himself?"

"No, of course not. I mean yes."

The Wiziratu sat silently and reviewed it, then concluded, "It is not a very interesting story." Both men were uncomfortable. The stumps they sat on had once been Manaca palms, the trees that the Warao Indians used to make their stilt villages. Unfortunately, Manaca was also the tree sought for "hearts of palm," a salad delicacy canned for export by the nearby CAPRO-DEL Corporation. The Indians were cutting all the manacas to sell to the factory, and there were no more left to cut. The villages were starting to fall apart. The owners of the factory now claimed to own the land, kept the Indians off, and tried to sell them boards to build their bridges, boards which unlike manaca poles, rotted. The Vicar felt that to be saved, the Indians would have to convert to Christianity.

Had the old shaman been able to speak like a European philosopher, he might have pointed out that Genesis started with a transcendent God, one that was apart from, separate from, a world that was a mass of disorder. God separated the chaos and made it orderly, from first to last, from larger to smaller. The Roaster and Frog, on the other hand, went from apparent order to disorder and back again, endlessly. For the Wiziratu, God was immanent, already pervasively in and amongst everything without time, so immanent, in fact, that God was not a separate concept but a transforming principle.

The transcendent God of the Vicar had served to make human life orderly for many years in desert cultures, and then in Roman Europe and America. But here, in the fragile delta, that same orderliness, made manifest in CAPRO-DEL (like all corporations, a structural replica of the Christian Church) which menaced the life of 15,000 Warrao whose God was immanent in the palms whose hearts they ate, the anaconda and peccary, in the Woman Frog, No-Indian, and the relations between them. The Indian form of incorporation was better. For example, some tribes cremated a body when someone died, instead of burying the carcass for eventual resurrection by a transcendent God. They mixed the ashes with a gruel, and the whole tribe ate the mixture. This is immanence.

Unfortunately for the occasion, the Wiziratu didn't speak like a philosopher, but even if he had explained all this, the Vicar would simply have claimed that Jesus was both transcendent and immanent, which is, of course, a paradox, not a proof. And since the Vicar wasn't any better than the Wiziratu at discussing all this, they continued to sit with their hands on their knees and struggle.

"God had a son named Jesus," said the Vicar. "He came to earth to die for our sins."

The Wiziratu had no idea what sin meant, so he asked "Was Jesus a roaster? Did he have two wives?" "Well . . . " the Vicar, disturbed by his own inclination to translate his story into the terms of the shaman, said "He did tell his disciples – his tribe – to eat his flesh and drink his blood."

"After his body was burned, of course. "
"No, as we do food."

The Wiziratu recoiled. He had suspected all along that there was something savage about these people. "His wives, of course, refused to eat his body."

"He had no wives."

"Did those No-Wives eat his body?"

The Vicar was unable to continue. He knew God wanted him to be patient with these obstinate people, but today he was exhausted. "It is finished," he said. "I will come again to instruct you in a few days."

The Wiziratu was disappointed, since the story was finally beginning to make sense. The Vicar still needed instruction on some points, but the Wiziratu saw that his new friend was already getting into his motorboat. Soon the sound of its engine blended with the sound of the chainsaws cutting the last of the manaca palms for the salads of the rich. Fences and signs were going up, dividing the waters, separating the elect from the damned, the mine from the yours. Beautiful parrots and red siskins were being snared, separated from their jungle, to be sold shipped to America. At night, motorboats without lights sped down through the labyrinth of the Orinoco, laden with drugs. Sometimes they overturned Warao boats; sometimes they drowned the children.

The Wiziratu paddled slowly through the twilight back to his village. He wondered whether that Vicar ate flesh and drank blood back in his own village. He wondered whether Warao children were safe from these people. His wives would be making palm-cakes, now, and asking one another when he was coming with roast game. It was early dark. "Oowang, oowang," sang the frogs.

© 1988-1989 Friends Publishing Corporation, All Rights Reserved.
1989  Winner, Associated Church Press Award

# PART 3

# The Law of Return

## Mincing to Gloucester

Of the four sailboats I built in the course of my life, I'd have to admit that the Ramona, the very first, was the only one that really made people avert their eyes. It wasn't because of the workmanship, which was passable, but it had vertical square ends, and an off-center main and mizzen mast, which scared people. In an effort to be helpful, onlookers sometimes told us that the boat would not sail at all because it needed a sharp bow to pierce and divide the water, and because a mast could never be set off center. These folk, I told my grandchild, were the same people who would be alarmed if a dog ate cat food, and they'd tell you all the reasons why.

Once my son and granddaughter helped me get the boat launched and tied up at the dock, elder sailors with their hands clasped behind their backs would explain to us that the boat would fall over in the water because of the off-center masts. Never mind that the boat floated perfectly upright before their very eyes. In addition to its natural design flotation, we had melted five hundred pounds of lead tire weights to make a deep keel.

But once we launched the boat, and motored out into the river and hoisted the main and mizzen, the Ramona, square ends, asymmetrical masts and all, sailed splendidly, because she had been designed for function, not for convention.

She was born from the mind of an eccentric genius, the iconoclastic naval architect, Philip C. Bolger. I sometimes had fleeting thoughts of sailing to Gloucester, where he lived on his own boat, to see what he'd think of the job we did.

But that was another voyage I was never to set off on, possibly because the prospect of the ocean was too daunting, or, more likely, because Bolger himself was more daunting than the North Atlantic in winter, because he was an obvious straight man who wrote, in addition to aquatic material, strange novels said to include themes of bondage and Republican values. I never read it, but other fans of his naval designs said the novel was pretty bad.

So when I thought of Bolger, the Genius of Gloucester, I found it easier to imagine him, say, in high school, suave, slouching, knowing since birth what a four barrel carburetor was, and able to discuss women's breasts in fascinated detail. Whereas I, having grown up in East Texas wearing white socks and playing the marimba, wouldn't have noticed if girls had breasts or not. Phil Bolger probably snapped towels in the locker room, while I only dreamt that one day it would be me who handed out those towels to the naked dripping athletes. I wouldn't ask for the job, they'd insist that I take it. "All right, but I can't be held responsible if anything immoral happens."

The old tile shower room in my high school was about as close to water as a person could get down in Richardson

Texas. Sometimes you'd see a scorpion in a dark tile corner, attracted by the possibility of dampness. Our family, having moved there, was adjusting to all kinds of new things – sickening heat, perpetual dryness, people who said howdy all day, and hot dogs not the color of cooked meat but dyed bright red, the only kind of hot dogs you could get down there.

We had moved to East Texas like chronic immigrants, full of hope, but nobody had told us that we'd be landing on the tail end of a seven-year draught so severe that the water ran red like a Mosaic plague out of the faucets because it had to be piped down from the Red River in Oklahoma. We bought flat distilled water in 5-gallon carboys at a Dallas store called 7-11. We'd never heard of a store that stayed open from seven in the morning to eleven at night, every day. It all seemed so wild and out of control. Where we came from, stores didn't even open on Sabbath, and I thought Texas was breaking all the laws of nature. Walking past a local bar I noticed a sign requiring patrons to "check all your firearms at the door." Not just some of them, I guessed.

Richardson in our day was a very small cotton town, very hot in summer, a black-and-white study of East Texas in the 50s, distinguished by a rusty water tower and a large feed store. It was a racially segregated little town, with a small whites-only movie theater called the Ritz, and a Rexall Drug with soda fountain. The countryside was not built up, it was cotton fields, chickens and hogs. Some of the boys at the high school were definite farm boys, muscular, open-shirted farm boys with Brylcreem in their hair who drove cars they worked on themselves.

The area around Dallas was very dry terrain at best, and when we, the northern immigrants, appeared on the scene it hadn't rained there for a very long time. The cracked land

83

was full of gypsum veins protruding on end from the baked clay mud and dust. We caught horned toads that squirted blood from their eyes, and were told to be wary of a type of white caterpillar called Asp which had only to drop from a cottonwood tree onto your back and you were a goner. I didn't believe they existed because I knew an asp was a snake, but later in life I learned there was in fact a Mexican name for similar creatures: "*asotador*." Maybe I had just been lucky.

It was around 1957. Ours was probably the first suburban neighborhood built on the fringes of this undisturbed world, little ranch houses set on the edge of a dried up lake bed which nobody realized could go under water because the draught had been going on for seven years. We moved into one of these subdivision houses, which were thirteen miles by bus, I believe, from my country high school.

The houses were not alike, nor impractical, but everyone focused on their twin-mimosa-treed lawns, which were exactly alike, growing either St. Augustine or Bermuda grass which turned brown in winter. The rich folk in our neighborhood had their lawns sprayed green, which at that time was only effective until rain, which did eventually come, causing the streets to run with green dye and the lake-bed lawns to sprout hollow mud towers built overnight by huge red and blue crawdads.

Next to our subdivision was a woods with pecan trees and huge live-oaks upon which grew parasitic mistletoe in the high branches. The pecans and mistletoe gave us extra cash at holidays. Naturally, I went too far afield hunting it and eventually discovered a whole forbidden world on the other side of the pecan woods. Tucked away there was a black community called Little Egypt, an actual freedman allotment that was home to many poor and extremely quiet families. I saw it, watched hidden from the woods like a spying gnome, but didn't go over there until the next summer, when the draught was still on.

It so happened that one very hot July day a wrinkled and sick elderly black man, a Mr. Hill, came to our front door with a bucket, asking for water. On my mother's stern orders, I helped him carry that and another bucketful back to Little Egypt. Mom, a Democrat, was furious that anyone would ever have to go beg for water. Obviously none of our neighbors closer to Mr. Hill's home had offered him any, either.

The families at Egypt lived in shanties and grew their own food, self sufficient but now their wells had gone dry. They didn't interact with the nearby white world, but the kindly people I met there in Little Egypt let me come around, maybe because I was so small and guileless, obviously in need of human contact. But I made everyone nervous.

During that summer I also worked in the afternoons up the hill at our local pharmacy, painting elegant window signs and working the cash register. I was also ordered to wait on any black customers who might cross the road from Egypt Baptist Temple, a ramshackle wood building that also held a classroom, the only part of the community visible from the highway. If a black person came across to the drugstore for medicine, he had to stand outside in the heat, and I had to go out, take his order, then go inside with his money and get him what he wanted.

I don't know how I ever consented to do this, but it was my first job and I was scared. The first two times I was told to go out and get the money I complied, ashamed of myself, but the third time was different, because by then I had met Mr. Hill over in Egypt, so when it was he who came across the road one afternoon I was unwilling to make him endure the humiliation of waiting outside in the deadly Dallas heat while I went in to get his bottle of medicine called Black

Draught. I asked him to please come in. He seemed frightened but he was sick, so he did come in where it was cool.

The owner of the drugstore, who wore purplish makeup and glitter eyelids and gave cosmetology classes at her counter, spied him from the back of the store. She stalked up to the front with a perfume bottle, spraying all around, staggering and gagging, saying "What's that awful smell?" She glared at me, and made me put his money in an envelope so she could get it to the bank without touching it. Shortly after that she cut my hours and then fired me.

Egypt, from then on, became a place of safety for me, not because I was there so much, I wasn't, but in my mind it was an oasis. When the white neighborhood kids figured out that I was gay and stopped acknowledging me altogether, I went back to Egypt and learned from one of the boys there how to fish a little and catch crawdads. I heard a lot of great gospel music in Egypt Temple Baptist Church and to this day will stop anywhere to hear black gospel. I'd like to think most folks would.

Of course when September came, I still had to get on the school bus with the other white kids. On the road out to Richardson I came to realize there existed other unnoticed black families, living off alone on the cotton plantings. Every morning our school bus passed one particular shanty, back in a cotton field on the last curve, called the Big Curve, before you entered Richardson proper. Every morning six tiny little kids in rags would stand outside it, giving us all the finger as we passed. I was beginning to understand why.

At school, stepping off the bus, we changed worlds. Richardson High was like any one-story pipe-rack brick school in any town of those times. The lunchroom offered Texas food served by white ladies in hair nets, sometimes including things like tamales wrapped in paper, or chess pie for dessert.

The Cafetorium was also used for performances, but in years past the school had used another building down the street, a white wooden Grange Hall. In our day it was still used for important theatrical events. Once, we put on Uncle Tom's Cabin with dead angelic Little Eva being pulled up into the flies on a rope. The play was popular, but the 'Colored' themselves were not allowed to see it there, or in any other school facilities. However they were given our worn out band uniforms and textbooks, and allowed to use the football field once a week.

The teachers in our school were not necessarily ready for an influx of relatively sophisticated newcomer kids, some from Texas, many from the north, but our families had been drawn there by the economics. Some teachers didn't like us, period. The biology teacher, Mr. Edge, was one. He taught that if you put a hair from a horse's tail into a flask of water, it would change into a worm overnight. He had seen it himself, he said. It never occurred to him that we might try it out. His was Republican science.

He also once gave me a jar with a live baby snake he wanted preserved as a specimen. He asked me to snatch it from a jar with some tongs and stick it headfirst into a flask of formaldehyde. The honor was mine, he said, because I was an officer of the Bio-Sci Club. He didn't mention what kind of snake it was, just hastily left the room, his face pale, while I did the deed. I later learned it was a copperhead, and that they are deadly poisonous at birth. Ah, Mr. Edge. He taught us that evolution was a lie.

On the other hand, our English teacher was Bettye Martin (with the e) who seemed to me an old-south tragic heroine, trapped in the classroom. She'd sigh at our interpretations of Silas Marner or our northern critiques of

Vachel Lindsay's poem 'Then I Saw the Congo" and she would always wearily return my creative writing assignments with a note of regret. She said they were very good but not what she had assigned.

The thing I liked most about her class, though, was being next to the Ag room. I always looked for excuses to go out and pass by the door and see the farm boys with their muscles, all of them attentively learning how to castrate sheep with berdizos. Once I somehow conned my way into a field trip with them to the Owens Country Sausage plant, where we watched screaming hogs get hit over the head with a sledgehammer.

Another time, when my mother got mad at me and made me walk the thirteen miles to school, I got picked up by one of the Ag boys, who showed me photos of Mexican prostitutes he had met on a weekend trip to the border. He seemed to know that my interest would only be pedagogical, but he didn't care at all. That was a ride I would always remember. In fact when an old classmate told me forty years later how that boy had died by electrocution, I cried.

For us suburban kids, with no sheep to castrate, there wasn't much to do. Ours was a world of arena roller skating, with live organist and mirrored ball, the conductor calling out "Couples Only!" or "All Skate!" We dressed in penny loafers with actual pennies in them and we used pink wax on our brush-cuts so the front stood up. We were easily embarrassed. I loved my school life. Home, though, was getting a lot more complicated.

It was odd, in retrospect, that a bunch of Dutch people would deliberately go live where there was no water. But at least our father had found a place close to White Rock Lake, which was almost totally dry then, a cracked moonlike expanse of hard mud, no vegetation. From the edge you could just barely see brown water, far away in the middle, like a distant cesspool. But when the rains came, it all filled up, unfolded, turned green, came back to life like the native resurrection plants.

Water was so scarce in Dallas in 1955 that they hired a rainmaker to shoot silver iodide from cannon into the occasional solitary passing cloud. Dr. Irving Krick, famous for supposedly forecasting the break in weather that made the Invasion of Normandy possible, was paid an enormous sum to make rain, but when he failed they ran him out of town.

My little brother knew other kids in the area because he played on a softball team. One day he showed me another swimming hole where they all went, a pond that didn't ever dry up. It was under big cottonwood trees out by Jack Evans' house on Audelia road. Good for swimming, but I was told you had to beat the water with branches to scare off water moccasins, which must have concentrated themselves in the only available water. They never did bite anyone, in fact Jack Evans apparently survived to become mayor of Dallas. He probably goes sailing on White Rock Lake, probably in a yacht, the sissy type with pointy ends, not square like those of Bolger's design.

And the only other body of water I knew of in Dallas was a river that had water but once a year. Sometimes we drove over it in our father's car and Dad would sarcastically say, "There's the Trinity River," but we'd see only a damp bed far below, and sometimes we would see ragged folk sticking their arms up into holes in the banks to pull out hibernating catfish. Sometimes, my father said, the fishers would yank out their arm and have a water moccasin clamped on their fingertips. You wouldn't catch me fishing that way. No sir.

Give me a good square boat and a lake to sail it in. Or give me a stack of dry towels, and make me a fisher of men.

Looking into the dirty pond water of East Texas I saw tiny black catfish with whiskers, wiggling at the bottom, and yes I could see why my Grandpa Achter said that every living thing of the land had its counterpart in the sea. But what about the crawdads, big and mud-blue, what on land resembled them? In the heat of an east Texas summer the answer was: scorpions. They too had legs on each side in serial homology.

And speaking of homology, were there any underwater queers, submarine fairies? Fifteen was the age to start 'thinking on that.' Was I myself of the God-created world, did I have a counterpart, or was I just a sport of nature?

The first person who had applied the word Fairy to me was a neighbor girl, Lynette, who got off the school bus at my corner. She smelled like a grown woman, and she carried her books to make her chest look more pronounced. Neither of these phenomena had any effect on me. I would not have noticed had not my friend Stanley pointed them out. To make an impression I walked beside her, but it was no different than if I had been walking beside an antelope. She said "Y'all know what yew are? A fruit flah. Fruit like a queee-ah and flah like a fairy. Now get away from heah."

I wasn't devastated, just perplexed, and glad there was nobody around to see what for a regular boy would have been humiliation. I still didn't understand that I was a queer. The other kids were getting wise, though. In fact, it turned out that everyone knew about it except me.

It was the band teacher who informed me, the day he couldn't control his anger at my fond attentions to another drummer, such that in the middle of a march he threw his baton over the clarinetists and trumpeters, so its cork handle bounced off my forehead. He shouted"Boy go do your courtin' somewhere else!" The whole band turned in their chairs to laugh. Next day he assigned me to play the tympani, which were located across the room, where I'd be alone.

I got him back, though at the annual spring concert at SMU. He had planned a fluty, delicate opening number, but as he closed his eyes and lifted his baton for the first note I let loose with my hardest mallets, bam boom. His bald head and face became tumescent again, so I lifted the back of my fingers to my lips in that limp-wristed gesture of "Oh dear, I must have made a mistake!" The concert never quite recovered. I had learned the queen's revenge.

* * *

And Yesterday

More and more newcomers from all over the country and all backgrounds had been settling in the outskirts of Dallas, moving in among the real Texans. The street where my Dad had bought us the new brick house was very different from the Dutch-only town we had originally come from. There were some Germans on our street, who my father didn't even nod to, and a Jewish family, who he liked but insulted behind their backs. And we had an authentic Texas family too, the Huffhines, who said "Howdy" to strangers and friends alike.

The Huffhines had three sons, all about my age, decent boys of somewhat goofy demeanor, who liked to tell us newcomers that they personally knew the Senator Johnson family of Texas. I believed them when they said they went with their father on weekends down to the LBJ Ranch in Johnson City, to visit the Senator and to court his two daughters. The brothers suggested with smirks and eyebrows that these Johnson girls were irresistible, and they implied that that Lucy and Linda were practically their brides-to-be. That was why they never went out with neighborhood girls: they were waiting for their Lucy and Linda to come back from Washington, which it seemed they never did. I grew unconvinced that Lyndon or Lady Bird even lived in Washington, or Johnson City either.

With a skepticism fueled by deceptions around my own identity, I nurtured a cruel wish to unmask these neighbor boys. In fact my wish to embarrass them probably gave me the extra push I needed to actually leave Texas for a few week that summer, to take a bus up to Washington D.C. I had decided that I wanted to call on Senator Johnson myself to see if this was all true. I didn't know that doing things like that were impossible.

Of course my real motive was to get away from my mother, who had stopped speaking to me altogether from the moment she confirmed my nature. When Dutch people get mad, they clam up and go sit in the barn. She just stayed in the house red-eyed, threw down the newspaper, burned the food and things like that. When circumstances required it she would talk about me to other people in my presence, making it seem as if she was talking to me. When we had a television to watch I dreaded the nights when Liberace came on to play the piano. My mother would turn to my father and say, "Look! I'll just bet he's a homosexual. He makes me sick."

I had heard that our next-door neighbor had a cousin who worked as a secretary in Lyndon Johnson's Washington office. So one day I went next door to ask about it, and the neighbor seemed to understand. Through a long distance phone call she arranged for her cousin to meet me if I went to D.C.

After school was out, the day came when my father, who was a kindly man but was afraid of my mother and would do anything she told him to, drove me in silence to the station to get my summer train north, back up toward Holland, Michigan, where he still had a no-good brother. From there, he said, I could use my own money to go wherever I wanted.

I was dressed in the hated gabardines and checked shirt that my mother had always bought me. She hadn't said goodbye, so it was up to my Dad. He did hug me when it was time to step up onto the train, and when I turned away from him I helplessly vomited on the conductor's brass-button jacket. My father ignored it and made me get on anyway. The conductor lifted my valise.

Visiting family in Grand Rapids was nice, but the travels after that involved mostly the stench of stale tobacco and disinfectant of bus stations in sketchy parts of rundown cities. The D.C. station didn't look much more promising than Chicago or Detroit, but my neighbor's cousin clearly stood out when I got there. She was much younger than I expected, the only person in the Greyhound station wearing business clothes, the only one walking in heels.

Hello, she said, an unusual expression for a Texan. She offered a gloved hand, the first I had ever felt. She made me feel wonderfully mature. We went in her car to a dark but elegant place called the Intrigue. Women didn't drive much in those days, not where we lived. Hardly a day passed without a joke about women drivers. But she drove expertly to the Intrigue, where, she said, secrets of State were traded, and John Kennedy was a regular.

I'd heard of him, but he wasn't there that night, nor were any other public figures. I was convinced, though, that the people who did sit there were all spies. They drank. I ordered a ginger ale, which I thought was a sophisticated request, and my neighbor's cousin did all she could to create an air of mystery for me, and then she dropped me at the YMCA to sleep.

At the Capitol building the next morning, it was a workday. We didn't have to follow tourists in lines or wait with the ordinary citizens. Because I was with my neighbor's cousin, we rode up on the Senators' own elevators from the coffee shop in the basement, and I got into the up elevator with Hubert Humphrey and Stuart Symington on their way to a roll call. This all seemed natural to me, I took it as a matter of course. What else would you expect when in Washington, except to meet Senators and such? I knew who they all were from Miss Darnell's class in Civics.

Hubert Humphrey was the only one in the elevator close to my height. He looked slightly down at me when I turned around in the elevator, fixing me with a look that made me think he might go to city parks at night.

My neighbor's cousin and I strode through the long halls, as she did a lot of pointing into offices and spieling off of explanations until we got back to the entrance to the Senate floor and entered the office right across from it. Lyndon Baines Johnson owned that one, the nicest office of all, because he was the Senate Majority Leader, the most powerful man in Congress.

Johnson was on the Senate floor at the moment, so my neighbor's cousin cautiously ushered me into his office as if we were apostates entering a cathedral. She continued whispering about different features, including his desk, which she claimed had been Abraham Lincoln's, built for knee room.

The office was an elegant green and gold with carpets and art works, and I hated to even sit on the chair as indicated. Then we just sat there in the corner in silence. It must have been half an hour. There was nothing in the room I hadn't studied carefully three or four times, trying to not be impatient. I wondered where Senator Johnson went to the bathroom.

Finally, the roll call must have been over and we heard people coming, so my neighbor's cousin put a finger to her lips to remind me, just as the hugely tall, very impressive Senator arrived, *en tourage*, with a great bustle of aides moving here and there. He carried a brown paper bag from which he helped himself to a piece of chicken as he sat and leaned back in the leather chair, putting his feet up.

He ate and he ignored us. He looked at some papers from the desk, and gave serious attention to the bone he was gnawing. Then out of nowhere his eyes were fixed on my guide. "Who's he?" he asked.

She said my name, mispronouncing it like "Shoon" the German way, and I started to correct her but caught myself.

"Why'd you bring him in here?"

"He's up from Dallas, Senator, to meet you. He's your constituent."

"Don't look old enough to vote."

She gave an accepting nod, and deferentially stood, ushering me toward the door. I felt myself blushing. That was it? He didn't even know me. I felt I had to do something, so I turned back and blurted "I'm friends with the Huffhines brothers!" Maybe he thought I was talking about the guys who rode bulls at the State Fair, because his last annoyed glance showed me he certainly didn't know anyone else by that name. So with that, we left.

In the car, on the way back to the bus terminal, I felt humiliated and stunned by his rudeness to me, and decided I would never again sit and wait more than fifteen minutes for any stranger. I've abided by that rule all my life. I also waited for the day when I could vote against Lyndon Johnson, but by the time I was old enough to vote he'd already been President one term, and had decided not to stand for a second one. Good thing, because I'd have voted no for sure.

Anyway, by that time LBJ was just another old straight guy to me. Who was he? compared to, say, Sal Mineo? Laughable old fool. Different species.

Hearing Southern talk again on the bus ride home was a comfort. I spent most of the night from Asheville to Texarkana imagining Lyndon Johnson scolding my mother on the phone, telling her she better take me back. In fact, my true mission, not the fantasy one, had been fully accomplished. I now felt sure that the Huffhines brothers must be liars, and couldn't wait to get back to tell them so.

# The Boys Sat Grimly There Alone

> Cats, totaling 30,000, have been
> eaten by hungry Parisians since the
> liberation. Acute food supply
> difficulties have produced something
> approaching a systematic cat hunt in
> the French metropolis. One cat is worth
> 30 shillings ($6.00) – 15 for meat, 15 for
> fur. In the poor districts they spend
> hours every day dangling a fishing line
> from the first or second floor windows
> at the end of which is a piece of cat's
> meat.
>
> Paris, Feb 11, 1945 (Reuters

Toward the end of his life my father regained his sense of smell. He had lost it years before, during the Second World War, either because it was burnt out by cannon smoke, or because something in him had just decided to stop smelling the death-miasma. His sniffer came back one day toward the end of his life when he lived near his daughter near the palmetto wetlands of North Florida. Suddenly he could smell the swamp.

Seated in a folding web chair outside his daughter's single-wide trailer, watching his grandsons climb a knotted rope up into a canopy of giant live-oaks, he told me he'd been thinking a lot about the World War. Part of his soul must have lingered around those battlegrounds of France, Belgium, and, most of all, our family's country of origin, Holland, where he had carried out the dead and wounded. But now he was sitting here in Spanish Moss cracker-house Florida, among egrets and manatees, drinking a cup of coffee.

We had all gone to town that day to see about getting him a flu shot. His doctor had declined to give him one, and, thinking it was because he couldn't pay, I was ready to go raise hell. But the doctor, a brusque and impatient man, just looked hard at my father, then took him into a back room. "Okay, I gave it to him." I asked if I could please speak to him privately and he took me in back. The doctor said "I didn't give him the flu shot because there's no point." I still didn't get it. "Can you tell me what my father's condition is?" He shook his head. "That's up to him."

"Is he able to understand?"

The doctor looked at me in amazement. "Do you have any idea how smart your father is?" he asked, and I just reflexively repeated one of Dad's own stock lines: "If he's so smart, why isn't he rich?" What an excruciating, stupid thing to say at such a moment, but it was what I said, and the doctor wasn't helping. Life was coming loose.

Dad was, in fact, very smart, smart enough to have chosen to live his life in a simple, plain manner. At eighty and under those live oaks he wore the same cheap linen plaid shirts and the same Sears shoes he'd worn all his life.

We were Dutch Calvinists, we believed in hardship, thrift, and predestination. It would explain why, when he was young, he had joined the army to get away from the Dutch enclave of Grand Rapids, but then, moved by destiny, had found himself two years later marching back into the Holland of his parents, fighting the Germans who had taken it over.

Back at his one-bedroom apartment in Gainesville, Dad and I paged one last time through his scrapbook of the war. One last time he traced the route of the 7th Armored Division, from Normandy up through the rest of France, then to Belgium and Holland and back south to fight the Battle of the Bulge and ultimately to cross the Rhine at Remagen and penetrate Germany.

The 7th Armored Division, the "Ghost Division," as the Germans called it, had contributed gallantly to the winning of World War II, landing on the Normandy beaches and not ceasing the northward march until 2260 miles later, when one of their tanks actually drove into the water of the Baltic Sea because it could go no further, because they had conquered all.

I asked my Dad why the 7th was called the Ghost Division. He pushed out his lower lip as he always did when thinking. "Not knowing, I cannot truthfully state." That said, he continued. "It's because we got assigned to one Army then another, even the British Army one time. The Jerries never knew where we'd show up."

"How do ten thousand men riding on tanks sneak up on somebody?"

This irritated him. "I don't know how to explain it. The world was different. People didn't think they knew everything. The world was bigger then. Even an army could hide."

"So did they let you to pick which division to be in?"

"No." He was showing me that I just couldn't understand. "The right to shop isn't in the Constitution, you know." He crossed his legs the other way and tried again. "After the war was already started they gathered a bunch of us green recruits, sent us out into the desert of California and made a new division out of us. That became the 7th Armored."

"Did you learn to shoot?"

"Yes. I never carried a gun in action, though."

"Why not?"

"Shooting tin cans is one thing."

That part I'd heard about. Clearly, his pacifism was one of the reasons he'd later been given some hopeless assignments on the battlefield. Army brass didn't appreciate a deliberately unarmed soldier. He was a seceder. It had gotten him into plenty of trouble, and I was realizing he had taught me by example to get into the same kind.

We kids had seen photos of Dad in maneuvers, living in a tent in the California desert. From those trainees the Ghost Division was formed from thin air, and the men, who thought that because of desert training they'd obviously be going to North Africa, were ordered to take a train to New York for the crossing to England. Their train went over the railroad bridge in Poughkeepsie, the bridge beneath which we now sail our boat in the Hudson.

My Dad's unit left on the ship from New York Harbor on D-Day, just as 3000 miles away the first American infantry soldiers were landing and being slaughtered on the beaches of Normandy. It was not until three months later that my Dad's outfit themselves crossed the English Channel to Normandy under a sky full of dirigibles, to regroup at on Omaha beach so they too could begin their own route northward.

And here they go.

The names of some of the battles and map locations in my father's scrapbook were familiar to me even in childhood because of the war comics my friends read, years after Dad had come back. There was Verdun, a crucial battleground in two world wars. The Battle of the Bulge. The Bridge at Remagen. I did not know that my father had been in all those battles. The Battle of the Bulge had kept German Troops from reaching a critical seaport. It was the turning point of the war. The Bridge at Remagen was the Rhine bridge needed by US and British troops to cross over to Germany, to victory.

Other boys went into raptures over the violent drawings in the comics, but war comics to me were just grotesque images, and my father was very aware of my lack of interest. He knew I was more distracted with trying to transplant jack-in-the-pulpits, violets, Dutchman's britches, catching tiny transparent crayfish and salamanders under rocks… he always knew who I was.

But he was still willing to go patiently through that old scrapbook one more time, in case I could somehow understand some truth it contained. Sitting with him in his apartment in Florida, as he watched the Weather Channel day and night, the cold fronts and warm fronts marching slowly from west to east, I realized that soon there would be no more chances to understand, that one day soon he would be carried out on a litter to his own predestined place in heaven. And oh how I would miss him.

# The Deugenits

*Grand Rapids, Michigan, 1915*

Benjamin Schoonbeek, my Dad's father, delivered mail from a horse wagon. Often, at the end of the day, he lifted up his tiny son, Bernard Earl, for a ride. The boy loved the horse and had always pled for a pony of his own, but it wasn't until his tenth Christmas morning that he awoke to find a small corral set up outside in the back yard, with manure on the snow within it. He ran out, looking around, then rushed back in, asking breathlessly where the pony was. His father said, "Well, I guess it got away. Don't crave after things of this world so much. A pony is not something to pray for." Welcome to Dutch Grand Rapids.

Dad's mother had also come from Seceder stock, so our Dad grew up attending church twice on Sunday and once on Wednesday night. There was Bible study, and they had ice cream Socials, if you can ever call a gathering of such northern Dutchmen "social."

My father knew all the hymns, and how to act pious. But there were many little clues that he'd really been what the Dutch called a "*deugeniets*," a ne'er do well.

Aunt Helen once confided to me that at age twelve my father had made an explosive out of a lead pipe and saltpeter gunpowder. He set it in a hole in the brick wall of his parents' porch, and blew it up. Dad, when he was 80, told me his parents never found out who did it, because he blamed the children of their Baptist neighbors, the Baptists having a surely undeserved reputation for violence back in Holland.

103

At about the same age, my Dad showed a pious side, even carving a wooden sign, later given to me, that said:

> *Three things a man must learn to do*
> *If he would make his record true.*
> *To think without confusion clearly,*
> *To love his fellow man sincerely*
> *To trust in heaven and God securely.*

I also learned from a family friend who liked to gossip that the famous right-whale skeleton which hangs even today from the ceiling of the Grand Rapids Natural History Museum had once been exhibited on the floor of the museum, but then had to be hoisted aloft out of reach after someone carved love initials into a rib bone. One set of those initials said "B.E.S." Not until his last days did my father confess that it was indeed he, Bernard Earl Schoonbeek, who had done it. He must have kept it a secret until then so our mother wouldn't see that the other initials weren't hers.

Those boys of 1914, the *deugeniets*, listened to the radio on crystal sets with earphones, and played wind-up Victrolas. Dad's school was let out just so everyone could see their first aeroplane fly overhead. For the rest of his life even a  massive 727 Jumbo Jet was still an aeroplane to him.

By the time he was a teenager my father drank, and he was fast with girls, but he also applied to Calvin College, determined to become a doctor, in spite of his *deugeniets* ways. He and Marion Ruth Achter finally got together after their high school graduations. Mom applied for a job at a certain carpet store because she knew Dad worked there, cleaning up the tile floors and shooting rats in the basement. He was soon walking her home after work before going to his night job, playing piano in bars. He was energetic, funny, and very smart. Marion and Earl fell in love. They never fell out of it.

By the time of his courtship, Dad was tinkering with his name, calling himself "B.E." for Bernard Earl. He never used his actual name, Bernard, because he believed people might think he was Jewish. At home he would look at his not-so-Dutch olive complexion in the mirror and lament, "Why did they give me a name like Bernard?"

He'd tried, apparently, to learn about his roots early on, but had gone about it only through the rules of wishful thinking. For example, there lived in Grand Rapids another family named Schoonbeck, but spelled with beck instead of beek. They were wealthy furniture manufacturers.

Dad must have pinned hopes on a family connection with them, but there was nothing to pin to. Even years later, when I called those furniture Schoonbecks to inquire, the respondents were hostile. "Ben the mail carrier? No relation!" slamming the phone down. (One should mention again that "beck" is a German spelling, whereas "beek" is the proper Dutch one, a significant detail to Hollanders.)

B.E., along with his much older brother Albert, his mom Jenny, and father Ben the Mail Carrier, lived in a dark house, which always smelled of the eggshells they saved in brown bags, and of mothballs and old sheet music. It was where the their two middle children had died, one from fever and one, they said, from self indulgence (eating cherries.)

On Sabbath, the noon meal, which had been cooked the day before, was preceded by the reading of a chapter of the Bible in English, solemnly and without inflection. It could take a long time.

After the cold dinner we would retire to the scratchy tufted nylon upholstery of the parlor, each male taking a turn to crank the round wood piano stool up or down and play a hymn. You weren't a man until you could play, so I caught on early that hymns were all basically the same three or four-chord pattern. The first hymn I learned was my grandpa's favorite, "Balm in Gilead," with only two chords. It made the wounded whole and healed the sin-sick soul. I pondered on what the bomb was made of.

There was, I have to admit, a simplicity and wholesomeness by which we Christian Reformed people lived. We were not supposed to dance, or to play cards, or to watch films except those that had no soundtrack. So instead we played games. Next to the piano was a square carom board half the size of a card table, with corner nets. It was identical to the game of pool, except that you flicked the caroms with your middle finger instead of poking a ball with a cue stick. One would never suggest, however, that there was any similarity between the two games. Likewise with cards. We played a game called Rook, which had 52 cards with pictures of various birds instead of hearts and clubs, a game which brought out all the same greed and killer instinct in the Christian Reformed as regular cards did with 40-gallon Baptists. But we were a better class of people.

And most of all there was the music. When Grandpa Ben went off to church, my Dad stayed home to play clandestine jazz clarinet to the hand-wound Victrola, and he could play a pretty fair stride piano too. He knew a song for every woman's name, every event, every condition. Say a word and he would start a song about it, and we kids loved it. His best song, and his closing number back when he played in barrooms, was a grand rendition of Sweet Georgia Brown, played in tenths. It always came after Sophisticated Lady, and it was the number we always requested in later years when he could be persuaded to sit at the home piano. So ingrained in my soul was his playing of that song that when he died I went grieving to the piano and sat down and played it, arpeggios and all, just the way he did. The experience was strange, because I had never actually learned the song, and could never play it again.

B.E. may have been a simple *deugenits* as a young man, but later in life there was always something deeper about him that made us ponder. He was remote, somewhere else, engaged in this world but not totally present, not even at the end as we sat there under the live oaks in Florida.  I had been coming to believe that it all had to do with the war, maybe having to come home from it to a wife he had once idealized but then didn't recognize, and to a four-year old son he hadn't even really met.

After discharge he'd gotten that job in Ohio as rug salesman, or rather a "floor covering representative", but he also became a full time alcoholic.

After my first brother Stephen died, four years further on, and my brother Philip was born, two years after that, Mom began to get some of her fight back. She revived.  She also decided, at the time of filling out the paper for brother Phil's birth certificate, that our surname would be changed to Schoonbeck, as if she wanted to become someone of her own invention, distinct from this man who'd come back from war.

My father was threateningly silent, because she knew very well that 'beck' was German while 'beek' was Dutch, but she famously said "Get rid of the beek or you'll be rid of me."

So he finally acquiesced, and, in the end, even he himself adopted the heretical spelling so we'd all have the same name. He became B.E. Schoonbeck, rationalizing that it gave him a sales advantage, since his new territory in Ohio was largely German. And if he needed it he always had that handy "Bernie."

How could he come back from a war against Germany and just move to a German neighborhood and assume a German surname? Even at the best of times, many Dutch people detested anything German. But my Mom had set the name change as her price for staying with him, a price that was very high. He saw her bet, and called.

In 1951 new wonders appeared in the world every day – frozen food, steam irons, our neighbor next door even bought a television set with a very tiny bluish-colored screen.

My father drove off to make his living, gone five days a week in a pale green Plymouth loaded with carpet samples, driving across the highways of Ohio, passing the fenced fields and windmill towers, calling at all the local rug shops, staying in motels, drinking to oblivion.

My father told me later that sometimes when he was out on the road at twilight he might see a tractor crossing the highway and think it was a tank with cannon. Once he slammed on the brakes so hard the books of carpet samples flew into the front seat, hitting him at the base of his skull, almost knocking him out. He said later that sometimes he actually did pass out while driving, but he kept it a secret so as not to lose his license.

When he was home, which was less and less frequently, my father would come in very late stinking of alcohol, and he and Mom would fight. My little brother and sister would sleep through it, but I would hear it. One night, after the roaring, my Dad broke down and I heard him say that he couldn't ever sleep, that when he slept sometimes he would see before him the piles of frozen bodies from the war, corpses that thawed out when the morning sun hit them, corpses making noises, and moving.

In our own mornings, all these things vanished from my child's mind, and I happily played army, wearing Dad's soldier cap shaped like an office envelope, and pinning his medals on my shirt. And there was a radium-dial clock he had taken from a downed German airplane, which I kept by my bed to see the green glow of the hand-painted numerals.

During the night, in the private life of our parents that only I saw, my Dad started having seizures.

He was checked into a hospital to have his skull opened and his brained probed with electrodes, unaware that he was being given an experimental procedure. Once he recovered and could wave from the hospital window, phenobarbitol and dilantin were prescribed. He took the meds, then and for the rest of his life, and never drank again. My mother was so out of control and hysterical that she too went for medical help for a hyperthyroid condition, which required surgery on her throat and a long recuperation. This all occupied my last grade school years, so I lost myself in books. The world of Henry Huggins and Dr. Doolittle became more real to me than anything in my own life. I constantly re-read the book on the explosion of the island of Krakatoa.

Finally, at the brink of divorce, Marion and Earl decided to start off fresh, and so, discharged from hospital and newly sober, Dad found a job as a rug peddler in faraway Texas. We got on a big plane, with four propellers, and headed south, served sandwiches with little paper umbrellas, and petits-fours for dessert as we gazed over the square fields of the farms, then the less cultivated land of the southwest, until finally we saw the barren desolation of East Texas, landing in the sketchy Love Field.

When my mother got off the plane the blast of hot air was so strong and terrible that she turned to get back on again. She wanted to go back to Grand Rapids, the phrase that would be endlessly repeated for the six years they were to live there.

Even in Texas, everything was informed by the war, it followed us there. Remembering desert maneuvers, Dad now instructed us to hold our shoes toe-upright in the morning and bang the heel on the floor, to knock out scorpions. It's something I still do, even now, living north on the banks of the Hudson. You never know.

Another caution had to do with where you pitched your tent. One morning he had awakened to find tank tracks that touched the edge of the tent, inches from the very place where his head had rested. He repeated that story when he was eighty, there under the live oaks, but I had just seen in the scrapbook a wartime Sad Sack cartoon showing exactly that scene, which made me wonder if this had really happened to him, or had he become confused?

That was before I was old enough to learn that a story has to change every time you tell it, because you always learn something from the telling that has to be included in the next retelling, and so it evolves, and becomes more, not less, true.

Still, there were pieces of his army tale that seemed absent and I didn't know what they were. That night, after I had driven him back to his little apartment in Gainesville and he had retired, at least for the few hours he ever slept, I got out the scrapbook and opened up a folded newspaper article that I hadn't paid attention to before. It was written in that wonderful 40's Walter Winchell prose. And a missing piece fell into place.

NEW YORK SUN, Dec 31, 1944
7th ARMORED ROSE TO GLORY BY ST. VITH STAND
*Held Off Panzers at Key Point in Drive to Split
American Lines Dec. 30*

They're all singing praise today for Soldiers of
the Seventh Armored Division – those oft-orphaned
waifs of the Western Front who have been bounced
from army to army and had their noses bloodied at
almost every turn.

For it was the Scrapping Seventh, slung into
the breach when Field Marshall von Runstedt's
spearhead was stabbing deeply into Belgium's side
ten days ago, which put the brakes on the Panzer
plunge and split the German penetration, forcing the
enemy to fight a two-way battle.

More than that, the boys sat grimly there
alone in the St. Vith sector, taking a mauling from
half a dozen German divisions, denying them the use
of that vital road junction, keeping them partly cut
off from supplies, and never letting them relax a
moment to fight elsewhere.

Commanded by Maj. Gen. Robert W.
Hasbrouck, Kingston, New York, and boasting as its
most famous guy the young Lieut. Will Rogers Jr.,
who is a popular platoon leader, the Seventh has
fought under four armies, British and American,
during its four months in combat. It fought through
Chateau Thierry and the Argonne Forest, encircled
Reims, and captured Verdun.

Somehow the Seventh always got hurt. The last big wound was late October when it was forced to hold a thin twenty five-mile line in the Weert sector of Holland and had to face the brunt of a German attack, which pounded plenty.

Officially the Seventh was ordered to hold the St.Vith sector for two days. It held for five, despite all that six surrounding Nazi divisions could do. Although officially they scrapped almost alone without outside help, the Seventh's troops actually accumulated one of the most savage little armies of soldiers ever seen on any front – straggling survivors of two semi-slaughtered units who had fought viciously their way back to that sector.

They formed a semi-circle front, fanning eastward around St. Vith, which forms the hub of a road network. Slowly the German power crushed all around the Seventh.

From almost every command post – normally far behind the combat line – combat command leaders literally could look at the battle a few hundred yards away at any time.

Finally after the fifth day the Seventh was ordered into a "Rest period." That only lasted a few hours. The boys went back into battle elsewhere."

During those five days that the frozen and weary 7th Armored Division held St. Vith and turned the tide of the war for good, my Dad and his platoon of ambulance medics rescued casualties from the front lines and brought them to a transfer station he'd set up in a St.Vith school. When the Americans were near to being overwhelmed by German tanks, their retreat out of St Vith began. But the gravely wounded under my dad's care were not to be the first to go.

The company commander, Al Williams M.D., was Dad's best friend. When the order came to move the wounded, Williams pulled my father aside and told him that some of the most gravely wounded would have to remain when the Germans came. They would be safe from harm under the laws of war. They would also require a medical officer to attend them, and so Williams had reluctantly assigned that job to Dad and his ambulance driver, Ezekiel, another Dutchman. They would be left there, in the evacuated, empty town of St. Vith, just Dad and Ezekiel, with fifteen mortally wounded soldiers, waiting, my Dad knew, for the Germans to come in and slaughter them all, just as they had recently shot all the wounded prisoners in the nearby battle of Malmedy.

During that black night, Dec. 30th, after the ground had frozen enough to support the weight of the tanks, General Clarke began the total retreat and evacuation of St. Vith. Against impossible odds the 7th had held the key town for five days, preventing the German army from traversing Belgium to reach the Atlantic port they needed to win the war, and now all the German rage and fury had gathered with guns and tanks aimed directly at that crucial little five-way crossroads.

My father and his driver sat there all night, til near dawn, listening to the last retreating American tanks clanking further and further off until there was nothing but stars and silence. "Ezekiel," my father asked, "do you know another way to get us out of here?" Yes. He had been scouting.

Dad thought again about the massacre at Malmedy and he made his decision. He collected all the morphine they had left and administered it to the wounded. Then he and Ezekiel loaded them into the two large lorry vehicles, and, against orders, they slowly bounced and rumbled across the frozen fields, out of the village of St. Vith, just as false dawn was rising. The light was sufficient for them to see what they now heard behind them: the German Tiger tanks, rolling toward the town, visible on the horizon.

Not all the casualties made that trip alive. Two died. My father had to tell himself they would not have made it anyway, but I think it was something he'd have to tell himself for the rest of his life. The others all lived to go home.

As far as the army was concerned, though, my father had disobeyed a direct order. Colonel Boyland, Commander of the Battalion, said, "I don't know whether to give you a reprimand or a medal." He gave him both. The reprimand was severe: my father was busted back to Sergeant and discharged from the armed services. But then immediately he was re-inducted. His former rank of lieutenant was restored in a Field Commission, a military honor, and he was awarded the bronze star medal for bravery.

Forty years later, in Florida, after his diagnosis of terminal cancer, B.E. Schoonbeck's first thought was to throw away his Dilantin and go on a long drunk. But then he thought of his grandchildren, and instead of drinking he just cleaned up the apartment, stowing away the few belongings he had left. Then he put on his hat and coat and waited for his daughter to drive him to the Hospice in Gainesville, Florida.

There, he took off the hat again, set it carefully on a nightstand, and hung his coat over the back of a chair. He insisted on dancing a few steps to the Muzac with the reluctant hospice nurse, who he called the Cherokee Princess because of her tattoos and feathers. And then he lay down.

While my father slept, my sister and I waited a long time for our brother to arrive from Michigan. Dad seemed to be trying to stay in the world long enough to say goodbye to our brother too, but neither he nor Philip made that last rendez-vous. By the time my brother was finally able to get there, Dad had already changed worlds. We three orphans made plans for his cremation, and left his body there while we all went back to his old apartment.

Brother Phil searched the desk drawers for a will, and he found one shortly, with a bankbook. Despite his poverty, Dad had guarded a few dollars for us. We also found a small box in his dresser drawer containing a medal, and newspaper articles describing the march of the 7th Armored Division. There was a clipping describing an event he had never mentioned to anyone: their subsequent liberation of a concentration camp at Buchenwald. I unfolded the delicate newsprint, and finally, confronted by images, let it dawn on me that our father's night screams, his talk of the piles of bodies, must have come from seeing Buchenwald itself, or a nearby camp. We had never known. He hadn't wanted us to.

**1,200 Yanks in German PW Camp Celebrate Arrival of Liberators**

*A portion of the Americans who escaped from Limburg camp to be found by the Seventh Armd. Div., First U.S. Army. (Other photo on Page 8.)*

B.E. Schoonbeck never learned, really, where in Holland his own forbears had come from, but the paradox that defined his life was that destiny, world events, brought him back to Holland, and to Belgium, to drive out the Germans. I don't think he ever pondered on the ironies, or the Calvinistic predestination features of his journey; he just lived it.

And it wasn't until I had become a Grandpa myself that I was able to locate the loose ends of the Schoonbeek line, following crippled Albert's voyage in reverse, back to the village he had come from, that tiny place on the north seacoast of Groningen province.

I think back to the beloved wooden houses of my childhood in Grand Rapids, of my Grandpa Jan Klaas Achter, sitting by the floor lamp with his newspaper. I think back to my other Grandpa Ben Schoonbeek the mailman, in his own scratchy chair, rocking back and forth as he read the Bible, davenning like a rabbi. I think of their Sabbath kitchen, the cold food, and I think of Sergeant Bernie Schoonbeek crossing the line into Holland before the Battle of the Bulge, maybe carrying with him the wishes of all the old Dutchmen who had left for America and never returned. Because Seceders always do return, you know. Just not in the same generation.

After the Battle of the Bulge my father's unit helped seize the bridge at Remagen, which enabled Allied troops to cross the Rhine and conquer Germany. And at some point further on he arrived at that camp at Buchenwald.

As we stared at the newspaper clip I knew it was at Buchenwald that the terrible physician Carl Vaernet had experimented on homosexuals, injecting people just like me with ground up glands and human hormones to make them "normal." Many had died; none had converted. Vaernet nevertheless, patented his injections to sell to American pharmaceutical companies before he finally fled incognito at war's end to Argentina, where the Nazi hunter Simon Weisenthal eventually got him.

The Buchenwald camps were liberated by the British, assisted by the American army, including my own father, who probably didn't have any idea that he himself was very likely part Jewish, and who certainly couldn't know that his first son would be a gay man. Unless, of course, there had been others like me in the family line?

The starved prisoners at Buchenwald were freed, all but the homosexuals. They – I want to say we – were sent by the Americans themselves to other prisons in Germany, to finish their 'criminal' sentences. I convince myself that B.E. Schoonbeek could never have cooperated in that injustice. I convince myself, but I don't know.

The war was over, and now so is my story of Marion and Earl, as they were known to all. Like Anyone and Someone, they had lived their lives as best they could, and suffered their own battles; they grew apart then together again at the end of it all. She died first, of smoking cigarettes, and he a couple of years later, of prostate cancer gone to the bone. Their ashes are buried in sandy soil beneath the thready grass of the Woodlawn Cemetery, in the place they were born, at Grand Rapids, Michigan, situate just to the east of a limitless body of water.

When my mother died we children had some polite disagreements about practical details. She had gone fairly delusional on her deathbed, thanking us one day for filling her room full of happy little children, the next day saying we shouldn't have taken her to such an expensive restaurant a few minutes ago. She asked for a Bible, to search for passages to be read at her funeral; she opened it upside down, and was shocked to see so many words. She said she wanted to be cremated in her red slippers, I suppose like Judy Garland.

Unfortunately she told this last request only to me, while I was sitting night vigil. My father and brother didn't believe that she had ever said it, or that she would have confided anything whatsoever to me because she didn't really like me. So they said she'd be cremated in whatever manner they determined, no red slippers. I was the *deugeniets* of the third generation, and not to be believed or included among those who count. Even in the midst of grieving I remembered when, as she waited for her first heart surgery, Mom had announced that she wanted to see everybody one last time before they wheeled her in. "Everyone except John." And that's the kind of thing that keeps a *deugeniets* in line.

Her power waned, though, once she really entered the hospital for that very last time. Knowing she was ready to die she turned her head toward me on the pillow and croaked out: "I'm sorry that we treated you badly all those years because you were... gay. We thought we were doing the right thing." Suddenly it was "we," though my father had never turned his back on me.

"Mom," I said, "I forgave you long ago, for my own sake. If you're sorry now, that's good for you! I'm glad."

She turned her head away. "Yes, I'm sorry," she declared to the wall.

Some time after she was dead, I had a chance to recall that last conversation in a phone call to my sister. "It's the truth," I told her, "Mom actually said 'I'm sorry.'"

My sister didn't exclaim in surprise; on the contrary, I heard her quietly laughing.

"Why are you laughing?" I asked.

"Because," my sister said, "she was lying."

Which, of course, was true.

When Mom's funeral plans were made, my brother came forward to take care of the gravestone. Though he sometimes had a hard time with emotional farewells, he was certainly better than me with the practical aspects. Dad had told him "When they carve her headstone, make sure the last name is spelled with the "b-e-e-k."

We were all silent, looking down. My brother balked and finally said "Mom wouldn't have liked that very much."

My father's voice was that of the army commander. "It was the name on the marriage certificate, and it will be the name on the grave." And it was, and it is.

A couple of years later, when my father died, I suggested to my sister that we should have his stone carved with the name ending in "beck." But that was just the voice of the family *deugeniets*, never to be taken seriously.

## Letter from Nijkerk

*Poughkeepsie, NY from Staphorst, Holland*

Dear President of Vassar College,

I am Willem Hoogesteger from Nijkerk NETHERLAND. Since a couple of years I had a good friend who's name is John Schoonbeek. He is a teacher at your college, but John's roots are in the Netherlands.

His forefathers came from my native village Staphorst, province of Overijssel. And did have a lot of correspondence about the Schoonbeek genealogy. But since a couple of months I couldn't reach him any more not by email and not by telephone.

It is my deep concern about John to write you this message. Please let me know if he is still living or something else. with the kindly regards of Anneke and Willem Hoogesteger from Nijkerk.

..........................................................

**Dear John, What do you want me to do with this?**
*Frances Fergusson, President, Vassar College*

..........................................................

Dear Fran,
Sorry, it's a Dutchman's way of expressing annoyance because I'm slow to reply. He knows I'm not dead. Please don't answer. (I'm Dutch too.) -John

■■■■■■■■■■■■■■■■■■■■■■■■■■■■■■■■■■■■■■■■■■■■■■■■

# Mine Tonight

*Vassar College talk, 11 October, 2006*

Back in 1968 at age 25 I lived in New York with a ragged Flemish poet named Marcel, an anxious, handsome man who chewed at his cuticles. We read Auden and Mayakovsky to each other, wrote our own bad lines, hoping they'd fool people who didn't know better. We went to see Charles Ludlam in "When Queens Collide" at the basement theater on the street that now bears his name. We drank at the Cedar Bar. We lived on the Lower East Side, a block from the Fillmore East, where we smoked pot and critiqued new musicians: The Doors, Jimi Hendrix and, most importantly we thought, the Vanilla Fudge.

There was one particular post-Fillmore morning when Marcel and I had finished up a dawn jog on a cinder track near the East River, and from there, still semi-jogging, we headed for our usual our 50 cent order of kasha varnishkes, buckwheat groats, at Aaron's restaurant on Avenue C. For some reason, on that morning I was especially weary of Marcel's table ponderings about girls, and so I let my glance wander, recognizing at the next table, also dining on kasha, the beat poet Allen Ginsburg and his boyfriend, Peter Orlovsky.

Ignoring Marcel, I chewed slowly, like an actor, trying to overhear their talk. It was about the boys of Tangiers, who, they seemed to be saying, were so available that they came down to meet the boat. Yes, well, I had covertly read my Gide, my Genet, I knew that North Africa was where literary homosexuals went. Maybe, I was thinking, they all really went to Tangiers, and just wrote "Tunis" to keep the real Shangri la a secret. Oh to be in a café, drinking mint tea, glancing at handsome boys instead of these repulsive poets, the woman-loving Marcel included.

Within weeks I had collected my money, sold my belongings, lent out the keys of my $40 flat, and bought a ticket for the slow freighter to Tangiers. The slower the better, I thought. I was so bored, like most young men who had just been through marching in civil rights, then marching against the Viet Nam war... After all the be-ins, the music renaissance, the St. Marks Poetry Project, Millennium films, the only thing that had kept me involved in real life was my job. Like many a homosexual before me I had sublimated my secret, troubling desires into chaste benevolent works, so, lacking even a degree to get a job, I had become a caretaker of delinquent adolescents, and in the five years during which I had devoted myself to that work the rough boys had changed me.

They lived twenty blocks uptown from my Lower East Side flat. The rowdy kids, almost all African-American, had their own rooms in a classy brownstone called Floyd Patterson House, named after the heavyweight champ who had once been one of them and had donated the building out of his fortune. He showed up to visit from time to time.

I'd been the nine to five leader of Group C for –how many years? Not so many, but still, it had been my entire adult life. To go off to Tangiers and leave the boys I'd known and loved since they were eight or ten would be wrenching, but I remained convinced that it was the right and necessary move. These were young men now – who I could love, and did, but could never even hug. In Tangiers I just knew I would meet a young man like me who I could love entirely. In Tangiers there'd be no ambiguity such as we lived with every day on the Lower East Side. The world there would be comprehensible, a world that even included homos like me.

But I had to get the six boys in my care back to their homes before I left. There were the Timmons twins, angelically identical, who had learned to stay in school and to stop breaking into houses; there was George, the desperately nearsighted boy with thick glasses who had routinely run away from home and ridden the subways for weeks at a time, squinting out the front window of the first car at onrushing track, until the police noticed and took him to court.

All the boys had court records, for truancy, thieving, drugs, assaults. They had done well with Patterson House's roof over their heads. All but one in my group had been approved for discharge. And once I started the serious planning, their Moms started showing up at the house with a bow tie, a jar of Dixie Peach, some new shoes.

With one foot out the door myself, I finally could see with great clarity that these boys had been taken from their homes because the courts believed their mothers were the cause of their problems, whereas actually their mothers were the main thing they had going for them. Their problems really came ultimately from institutional racism. The boys had bought the idea that they were bad, and they never fought the power, just each other. I wanted not to be part of it any more. They didn't need a white guy to look up to right then.

Before leaving the job, I decided to take the boys on one last adventure, to Washington D.C., thinking they might never see it if they didn't go now. My goodbye present. We would take a plane down, come back by bus. A rich woman who worked as a volunteer gave the money for fares. I couldn't take the littlest boy, Walter, who was too young and too wild. The six others were old enough to make some money on their own for the trip. That was the deal. They had to raise ten bucks. Several of them bought cans of shoe polish and hit the street. I got into trouble with the Director for condoning this, because it was considered demeaning and stereotypical, but I let them do it because I didn't know how else they were going to raise ten bucks legally in a hurry.

It's hard to describe the excitement and suspense hovering in the air when I left Patterson House for my own home the night before we were to leave. The boys all had their best clothes, their 'vines,' laid out, and had polished their own shoes. But at home when I woke at 3AM to pick them up for the early flight from LaGuardia, I heard on the clock radio that Martin Luther King had just been shot and killed. It was almost too much to take in. It was incomprehensible. Stunned, I headed for the house as planned, running on autopilot. The boys would still be wanting to go on the trip. Would that be right? I'd wait til I got to the house to decide what we'd do. My brain was going "What? What?"

The two night counselors at the house had already heard the news too, and I sat down with them. "These guys have saved for months for their trip, they worked for it," I said." But I don't know if we should go."

"Are you really considering it?" asked one man, incredulous but almost admiring.

"Well I need to know, do you think it would disrespect Dr. King if the kids went to Washington this morning?" I asked. "Maybe we can do something there to pay respects?"

"Yeah," said the other counselor very emphatically. "You should go." And so we did.

I told the boys the news about Dr. King and they were sad, but none had any intention of canceling the trip. In the taxi they were all able to recite together "Listen people while I sing, The story of Martha Lutha King" They didn't understand exactly why he was so important, but he was like George Washington on a dollar or somebody else distant and permanent. They were solely focused on going to Washington.

The plane ride was elegant, the boys were thrilled, the landing was easy. As we descended to Washington I noticed out the window a fair amount of smoke and thought, 'I didn't know there was so much industry here.' The boys were frightened of the descent, but they had all been able to endure it and had charmed the stewardesses.

We took a bus from the airport toward the Washington Monument. It was a beautiful April day, Friday morning, and no crowds at all to be seen. We had the Smithsonian almost to ourselves. We went to the FBI, the Capitol, the Pan American Building, and the White House. There were no lines.

I was careful not to betray puzzlement to the kids, but they noticed something wasn't right. When we came out of the White House to head for the monument, they wanted stop at a carousel, which none of them had ever ridden. But seeing these joyful young black men riding a carousel like little kids on a perfect spring day with no one else around to judge them made me cry. I decided it was the moment to call it a day and go back. The trip had been wonderful, it had been the right decision, they had learned a lot about their country. That's what I thought as my eyes followed the smoke rising north of where we were.

The older boys read my concern as we walked toward the bus station. "Why are you walking so fast?" There was a pungency in the air, an eerie quiet, and then, as we turned into the neighborhood near the terminal, there was sudden noise. There was smoke, glass breaking. "It's a riot!" George Jones cried happily. 'C'mon Scooback, let's get a TV!" They were ready to join the many other people running in the street.

"No, c'mon you guys. This is dangerous. Let's get to the bus."

"Dangerous? What, you scared?"

'Of course I'm scared."

"Why?"

"Because I'm white, for one thing."

George Jones looked at me horrified, his face that of a person betrayed. "I thought you told us you was Dutch!" Pointing at the skin on my arm  I shrugged, then after some resentful muttering amongst themselves all six boys formed a circle around me and walked me the rest of the way back through the smoke to the bus station, protecting me from any possible harm.

From the grey bus windows we saw flames, heard gunshots and glass breaking, Washington was burning. The driver must have been local because he careened through back streets and smoke and soon got us out of there, back onto the beltway, and on our way back to New York. The boys relaxed a little, but they were baleful, sorry that just because of me they couldn't go to the riot.

I wondered what we'd find in New York, too. I'd finally figured out that this was all about grief and rage at Dr. King's death, but as it turned out things were quiet in the city, at least where we lived. The boys fell exhaustedly back in their own welcome beds, after a trip that of course none of us would ever forget.

Those kids have had a lifetime in which to pay Dr. King homage, but that day might have been their only chance to see the White House and meet a Representative and ride a carousel. The dignified and noble way they handled the whole situation was a tribute in itself. They came back young men, eager to learn their own history.

By September the time had finally come for me to leave Patterson House and strike out on my own. Four boys now remained, three of them just days away from going home. But still there was Walter... the littlest one. I had known him since he was first sent upstate at age nine. His surname – Vandermeer – was Dutch like mine. I'm sure his father came from the Dutch colony of Surinam. Probably his forbears had been brought there in shackles by my forbears.

He was so tough, a demonstrative and provocative child, being watched over by me, a repressed white self-conscious, self-doubting semi-adult, but we hit it off. I had always delighted in Walter's sense of humor, and he had become very attached to me. Without wanting to, I had let it happen – real paternal attachment, two-way. With an eleven year old. Big mistake, but can you go on in life until you make your first big mistake?

Though he was the youngest and tiniest, the other boys on the group were afraid of Walter because he could fight, and because they said he was a faggot. I thought it was probably true that he was gay, (in those days we said "would be" gay, because we weren't supposed to believe a child could be born with that sensibility even though we knew we ourselves had been.)

So I had tried to keep a distance from him, so as not to be accused of "making" him gay. The last place a gay man would want to be tagged was at a Boys Residence. And any gay man in my position would dread getting constantly hugged by a little dynamo like Walt, or have him jump in my lap, but that's what he always did, a natural affinity.

And of course, it didn't really have anything to do with sex. The straight boys at the house always did in fact have some kind of sexual activity going on between themselves, which they called 'playing sex.' But more than once I heard one of the boys in Group C tell someone else, "Don't play sex with Walter. He likes it. He's really a faggot!"

Walter was not above playing upon their fears, either, nor on mine. Once during a house meeting where all boys and staff were present for some solemn moment, this innocent eleven year old came up behind me, grabbed my ass with both hands, and yelled "You _mines_ tonight, baby!"

It was with very conflicted feelings that I started the process of returning Walter to his Mom before I was due to leave, convincing myself that he belonged with her, up on W110th Street in Harlem. I could almost feel myself pushing off the responsibility onto her, though I knew she was overwhelmed by life.

The night before I was to leave for Tangiers, little Walter got one of the older kids to show him how to get to my packed-up apartment down on 6th Street. The bell rang. I opened the door a little ways and looked down. There he stood, looking forlornly at his shoes. He said, "Can I come in?"

I tried to sound stern. "Walter, you're supposed to be uptown at your mother's this weekend. How'd you get down here? Who told you where I live? You know I'm not going to be working at the house any more."

"But I want to go with you." Oh man. I never expected that. This kid was something. I still wasn't aware then that I was doing this whole Tangiers thing in part to get away from kids like him, the responsibility, the attachment. But yeah, something fatherly in me wanted to take him too.

"I'll be back, Walt. I'll find you." He raised his head and his weeping eyes glittered at me. "You a *damn* liar," he said quietly. He was right.

I knelt down and hugged him as he resisted, folded some dollar bills into his shirt pocket for the subway home. He just left his arms at his sides, we both cried, me kind of hating myself for failing in courage, sanctimoniously telling myself it was for his own good. He wanted to be Mines Tonight, and in a better world I could have been his Dad, try to be even a better one than mine was to me. His own father had long ago been deported and then murdered. But the old feeling came over me, the feeling of 'run for safety' that every gay man knows, and I closed the door while he still stood there. I closed the door.

The next morning I waited very alone at the rail of the old ship that smelled of fresh paint. As the ship's horn blew there appeared below on the pier the tiny figures of the new counselor, and the three other boys from my group who had come to wave farewell. Three, not four. Like the other passengers, I held one end of a roll of crepe paper given to me, and threw the rest of the roll down to the boys, so that as the ship pulled away they could keep the paper unrolling and stretching until the connection had to break.

As long as I live, I will never forget, after two weeks at sea in the listing, rusting freighter of the Yugo line, the smell of land, the smell of Africa. Before we even touched shore, I could discern that Ginsburg had told the truth – the hustlers did come down to meet the boat. Some were flyblown, one-eyed, crippled, and starving, some were stunning, even much handsomer than the ideals of my imagination. I hid my face and lowered my eyes.

133

For several months I sat in cafes drinking mint tea, smoking kif, writing ideas on lined paper. On one occasion I sat nervously beside Jean Genet at the Café de Paris in the Socco Chico, and once I was present at a sighting of William Burroughs, which was a pastime of disappointed writers in Tangiers then. But otherwise I could claim nothing literary. My notebooks may as well have been blank.

Then, eventually I did start to hang out with some street hustlers, wanting not to hire them but to pretend I could be one of them. They were good sports and taught me to stay stoned on kif all the time as long as I did the buying. I loved to sit in cafes where there was night drumming and sometimes djilala dancing boys. I learned a little Arabic, and observed Ramadan. One boy from the blab school I went to took a liking to me, and brought me harira soup to break the fast every night of Ramadan, lingering after we were done eating, but I didn't like him. He had flaws. I would have to search for someone more perfect.

Months later, flat out of money, I again turned up my collar and rushed down to the monthly Yugo freighter, this time listing its way in the other direction, back toward the Red Hook shipyards in Brooklyn.

Halfway across the North Atlantic a winter storm came up and blew us almost all the way back to Portugal. The stewards wet the tablecloths so the plates wouldn't slide, and they filled the wine decanters only half full. We few passengers had plenty of kif – only drug traders took the freighters in those days – so we spent nights in the officer's saloon looking back at the wake, watching the moon leap and circle as if it, and not the ship, were moving. The lopsided freighter was being tossed so high that its single propeller came out of the water and shuddered the entire vessel. We could have sunk and nearly did, but it wouldn't have mattered. Not to me.

Back in New York, broke and still determined to be a writer, I went to a 42nd Street employment agency, thinking to get a job delivering sandwiches. Also, I had heard that 42nd Street was where street hustlers hung out in the city. But I didn't see any hustlers. The agent asked if I would like a job 'in publishing' so of course I said sure. To my amazement, they sent me to the Time-Life Building, where I was offered a job as a copy boy.

The work consisted of rolling up typed onionskin stories and sticking them into a plastic capsule, which was drawn up into a network of constantly sucking pneumatic tubes. You could hear it rattling into the distance, and the change in air pressure would tell you when it had been coughed out to another copy boy on another floor. The copy inside was then hand-delivered or forwarded to another station. That was my job, sending things through the tubes, putting stories on editors' desks, and once in a while going out to get the important people lunch.

The Time job was most intriguing when I could quickly read the stories and memos as I carried them down the hall. So, with only a few weeks under my belt, I was able to learn that a big story was in the works – a cover story – on homosexuality, a topic that had never seen major media print before.

I was embarrassed just reading about it, and hoped nobody saw me expressing interest in the topic. It seemed that earlier in the year, there had been some sort of transvestite riot at a bar called The Stonewall. Over the next week I tried to piece together the story myself. And through assiduous memo pilfering, I realized that the suit-and-tie Time-Life reporters were sending lame excuses to the Behavior editor about why they couldn't work on the project. Most of the notes included the word "wife" or "girlfriend" (The reporters and editors were all men then, in offices with windows, and the fact-checkers were all women, stationed in windowless cubicles.)

My curiosity overcame me, so one evening I took a breath and marched into the Behavior editor's office and offered to go downtown myself and get some stories. The editor, named Chris Corey, asked to see some of my writing. On the strength of what I gave him, he issued me a press card, which would be a great trophy to show my parents, but more to the point it would give me perfect cover to observe the homosexual world I had heard and read about. I'd be able to see everything, go anywhere, without the burden of being assumed to be a homosexual. Maybe I'd even meet someone good enough for me.

Out of all the interviews I did for that story, after all the visits to gay bars and meetings in church basements, of all the drag queens and street hustlers and desperate aunties I talked to, there was one man who seemed to speak to my own situation, a guy named Marty Robinson, who looked and acted like any other person, a carpenter by trade, a handsome man, who explained to me that the new concept, called "gay," referred to the whole person, not just sexuality. Until then I had only heard the term "homosexual" or "queer" used as a noun, which fit like my mother's gabardines, and located my identity exclusively in sex rather than love and sensibility.

But more important, I did feel that I was different from, say, the athletes of my high school in every possible way – same species, different varieties. I knew instinctively that somebody like Marty Robinson would be likely to laugh at the same things I did, as straight guys would wonder suspiciously why we were laughing.

At first I hated the word Gay, which until that time had been used mainly as a code word among older people who were wise to the culture. "It'll be a gala event," meant it would be for Gentlemen of Distinction Only. But now I was being sold a new and deliberate meaning of Gay that said: this is who I am, was, and will be; this is central to everything about me, whether I'm sexually active or celibate, whether I'm gendered or not, alone or with someone. When I made myself say "gay" it was like Popeye saying, 'I yam what I yam,' and eventually I would come to like who I was.

Along with this Gay word came the concept of Coming Out, originally a ridiculing reference to debutantes, a phrase used by the drag queens who scorned anyone who hid their real identities in the closet with their gowns. Of course drag queens believed that all gay men secretly longed to be girls and wear sequins, whereas in fact regular gay men then wanted nothing more than to be disassociated from the drag queens. But we didn't mind borrowing from their scalding wit, or their vocabulary. With the advent of the gay movement, the term Coming Out came to mean forming or discovering a definition of yourself, and then revealing it to your friends, and finally to your family. I reluctantly started to become a gay man. Not A Gay, which sounded to me a lot like A Queer. Just a gay man. Back then, homos of both sexes were still believed to be people confused or oppositional about their gender. We radicals didn't believe that at all. We knew that a lot of drag queen friends who came to the bars to make entrances weren't there to meet men, they were there to wear pumps. Theirs was the gender discourse; being gay men was something totally different.

This sudden personal transformation, from closeted queer to 'out' gay man, had an effect on the story I was filing for Time Magazine, giving it at least some authentic historical grounding, a location in a social context. The experience of reporting had also paid off in terms of my personal education.

The story was a hit with the editors. It was group journalism then, so reports had come in from everywhere and none of my material made it whole into the final story. My point of view had made an impact, though: the Behavior editor liked what I wrote, so I was soon taken off the copy desk and assigned upstairs to do more reporting for Time's New York Bureau, working for the bureau chief, legendary Viet Nam journalist Frank McCulloch.

The day after the gay story ran I arrived to find the Time-Life Building being picketed by some of the very men I had just interviewed downtown at Gay Liberation Front. I ducked and walked a block around to use another entrance. To be sure, the final article that Time had run had been edited into its usual kind of snide editorialized prose, but the story wasn't that bad for 1969. And it was the first one ever done on the subject! A national cover story! Nonetheless, I was already beginning to realize that there was a decision ahead for me.

Frank, the bureau chief, who was bald and actually used an editor's green eyeshade, gave me an In box, with my name on it. On that first day on the job there was a fresh new assignment in it, my second story ever, with a note saying, "John I have a hunch you might be good with this."

It was a clip from that morning's New York Daily News. It said "World's youngest heroin addict dies at age 12." Before I even got to the end of that headline an awful fear and dread came into me, and I read one word at a time without looking ahead because I knew it might say the impossible, the inevitable... Michael Baden, New York coroner, had announced that Walter Vandermeer, age 12, had died of an overdose of heroin last night in a tenement in East Harlem, the youngest person to die in the current epidemic.

It was my Walter, the boy I had denied and left behind, the one everyone had said was gay. Sitting there stunned, unable even to think, I told Frank "I know him."

He grinned and said "I knew I had a good hunch about it." But when he saw my face he turned away. I couldn't think of how to explain to him and didn't try. I just put it all into the story, sick in my heart. It ran that week, this time with my byline, in the front of the book in the Nation section. Millions of people read it. And then I was interviewed for the New York Times by the great journalists Charlayne Hunter and Joe Lelyveld, and I talked on television shows, inwardly bewildered, grieving, responsible, confused, unable to work or talk to anyone, wishing to die.

In retrospect, I know that it was out of that terrible experience that I was given an awakening, not with a big eureka, but more like a lens turning into focus. I would no longer keep silent when others assumed I was straight, that was the first thing I decided. I'd never again allow people to define "gay" by their own imaginations about sex, but rather only by my reality of love and sensibility. It is who and what you love that's at the heart of who is gay; the sexual expression is just a confirmation, and not even a necesssary one. All at once I wanted to become a defiant, strong gay man, to initiate change, not just react to other people's mistaken ideas. I vowed to step up to protect young gay men and boys, and young lesbians too, from the dangers that I had always thought were our natural due. I knew it would get me into trouble, but it was exactly the kind of trouble I wanted.

This was the first time I'd ever felt there was a reason for me to be in the world. I was not just here by mistake, as an uninvited guest. Out of cowardice I had failed Walter, and would always grieve for that, but finally I realized that like all gay men I was a necessary player in the concert of life.

Millions more boys would be born with gay sensibility in years to come, and who would protect them if not us gay men? We'd have to lay aside our fears of being hated by straight people, the realistic fears of innuendo, of accusation and blackmail. I had an obligation to get strong enough to provide to at least some of those courageous boys the care and protection they deserved. For I was nearing thirty, and now the time had come, to take my place and do the work that God ordained be done.

# Why The Shad Come Back

Let spring come to the Hudson Valley, and everyone acts as if they can't wait to get some shad roe. Well, not everyone. "Either you like it or you don't," says Andy Vlamis, proprietor of the College Diner in New Paltz, NY. "Me, I don't." For those who don't like it, Shad roe consists of two glandular pouches of grainy, claylike material ("like wet sand, with a fishy smell," Andy explains,) wrapped in bacon and served fried over toast. Each pair of these delicacies contains some thousands of fish eggs.

One of New Paltz's best-known waitresses, Bert DiLorenzo, has been dishing it out at the Diner for twenty-eight years. "People love it, hon," she says. "I love it myself." Her colleague, Shirley, shakes her head. "Folks do order it, but I usually wrap it in foil to take home, especially when it's for the ladies." One asks: if the ladies don't like shad roe or can't eat it, then why do they order it? For fertility?

The proprietor of another diner thinks he has the key. "People eat roe because the rest of the fish is no good," he says, without explaining why the fish is then caught in the first place. "When I bought this diner the local fishermen talked me into buying about fifty pounds of shad roe. Maybe I'll help them out, I said. Well, I served two orders. The rest went in the garbage. It isn't a big money-maker." Did he eat some? "One of the two orders. I guess some people like it – the people who go to fancy restaurants," he said, with a baleful look across the parking lot at Coppolas. "But I don't."

143

Then who does? One aficionado, so to speak, Dr. Charles Spalding, a psychiatrist in Garrison, who this year put away two platters of "Lungs'" as the roe is called on his side of the river, feels that eating shad roe has a primal, ritualistic quality. "It's what you're supposed to do in the Hudson Valley," he says. "Probably the Indians ate shad roe. But what I really like about it, to tell you the truth, is the bacon."

Spalding's colleague, Judith Weiner-Davis, only eats shad roe in French bistros. (What does she ask for, *les enfants premature du poisson*?) She says "It reminds me of liver. Or no… a mild, fishlike pate." Ms. Weiner-Davis tasted her first morsel just this year, and intends to go back for more of the high-class stuff. She, too, has a theory about why people eat it, something to do with ovaries and cannibals. "Anyway," says Weiner-Davis, "talk to my gynecologist. I once asked him whether shad roe might be toxic to fetuses, but he said the river is clean, and anyway shad don't feed in the river. He declared that he would eat shad roe every year, and the day he didn't eat it would be the day he died. I started going to a different gynecologist."

Although not everybody likes its taste (and never mind the morals of dining on souls of the aquatic unborn), shad roe, and the annual rite of consuming it, goes on; corporate fish dealers sold more than ever this year. Yet Frank Parslow, of Port Ewen, who has been a shad fisherman for forty-four years, says this was his worst season. "The fish didn't come up the Hudson, or the Connecticut or Delaware," he says. "I used to get over twenty tons of fish in a season, but this year I didn't get a quarter of that." Not because of pollution, either. While some fishermen attribute the small catch to the proliferation of unfishable striped bass, Parslow has a different theory. "The big shad school starts moving up the coast from Florida around Christmas," he says. "The first catch is at Indian River. By the time they get to the Chesapeake, a set of roe is bringing nine dollars. And there's still plenty of fish . . . until they're due to come up the Hudson.

"1 think what is happening is this: there are boats off the coast of Jersey. By the time the school reaches Jersey the big boats just get all the shad. If I knew next season was going to be like this one, I wouldn't even start."

Most of the fishers on the river are older men, and some are going out of the business. It is not unusual in the Hudson Valley to lament this fact, whether you eat shad or not. Parslow's son, he says, owns a nice fishing outfit, but he works at IBM. His grandson, too, once loved to go out for shad in the spring, but last spring's building frenzy provided him with what he hoped would be a more sustaining job as a logger and bulldozer operator.

And so a certain way of life is in jeopardy, and not just the colorful life of the fishermen. Eating shad roe in the spring is one of those rituals that keeps us who we are; it goes very deep into our history and way of belonging. Sometimes we pretend to believe that the value of a thing depends only on whether it gives one person the advantage over another. But when you look at how we really live, we do a lot of things that don't make that kind of sense. And the impractical things in our lives usually turn out to be the very things that keep us connected to each other. Why else would a restaurant proprietor buy fifty pounds of shad roe from his neighbor every year when he could only resell a little? And why else would local ladies so good-naturedly go along with this spring fertility rite of eating fish eggs?

Trawlers will fish the Jersey coast until the shad are gone, and then they'll go somewhere else. Strangers will buy condos on the river shore and eat Swanson dinners in the spring, never really becoming part of the communities they live in. But what about us indigenous Hudson Valley folk? We'll still be here, and those who belong will eat shad roe, whether they like it or not.

This spring, I went to the College Diner to live up to my responsibility. Bert DiLorenzo was just going off duty, and Shirley took care of my booth. "Here you go," she announced like a hangman, sliding the heavy platter before me. It looked almost attractive, like afterbirth with curlicued carrots and slices of lemon. I ate the carrots, and picked with the tine of a fork at the bags of roe, trying to work up the indignation to eat it by imagining huge foreign trawlers taking away the birthright of the fishermen's grandsons. Why, those people had no right to eat up all our shad roe! What if my own son should be unable to eat shad roe in his time?

The truth is, my son was out in the foyer playing video games, and wouldn't have eaten shad roe if you paid him in quarters. In fact, I thought I should go out to see how he was doing, while I considered all these aspects.

I really wasn't out there that long, but before I knew it, Shirley was at the door, smirking slightly and holding out a brown paper bag to me. "See?" she said. "Nice try."

"No, it was delicious," I apologized. "There's just so much of it." "Sure," she said, with a serene look, a woman who would not be fooled. Guilty, I drove home, put some Swanson dinners in the microwave, and unwrapped the shad roe. Then, speculating on whether it was ethical for man to so divert the food chain, I served it to my dog, as hundreds of other Hudson Valley people had no doubt done this year. Who knows, maybe the Indians did the same thing with their shad roe. Maybe their dogs even ate it. As for mine, well he's a little picky. But believe me, he really liked the bacon.

© 1990 Upriver/Downriver Publications

# A Simple Gift

Sometime in the 1960s I was working as an orderly at Rusk Institute, a rehabilitation hospital in New York, where I met a charming old Swiss man, very short, his tweed cap concealing a head injury, his now-useless left arm in a sling and a cane in his right hand. Fritz was there to learn to walk again after suffering brain injury in an accident aboard a ship. Speaking was difficult for him, but he always wanted to talk with me while he did his exercizes. He told me he was a painter. I assumed he had painted the decks on the ship, or perhaps he just painted people's garages.

My task in the rehab room was to accompany Fritz up and down the halls twice a day as he re-learned to put one foot in front of the other and keep his balance. As the weeks went on, his speech improved and we had many friendly talks. I looked forward to his wheelchair entrances, as he slowly pulled with his one good foot on the floor while pushing the wheel of the chair ahead with his one good hand.

Fritz had been there several weeks before he finally told me how his accident had happened. He was crossing the

Atlantic on the ship Michaelangelo, he said. There was a terrible storm, during which he was thrown across the dining room, and had broken his skull.

I knew that garage painters didn't travel on elegant ships like the Michaelangelo. Who exactly was this man? With some reluctance he confessed to me that he was in fact a painter of canvases, an artist. I thought at once of florals on black velvet, State Fair portraits.

So Art became the topic of the day as we walked, and I took the opportunity to explain to him, day after day, about light and color and Dutch artists. He usually showed a delighted little smile when I lectured, but one day, when I mentioned the Dutch artist Piet Mondrian, he burst into tears. I assumed he was just very tired.

Fritz still had the use of that right hand, and he always hoped for more recovery, but after a few more weeks his medical insurance ran out and he learned that he had to go home before he was fully recovered. I stayed by his side constantly in those last days, until it was time to bid him adieu at the hospital door. He took a long time to wheel himself out to the threshhold, where he locked his wheelchair and with one hand pushed himself up out of it, now without assistance. Then he faced the open door and shuffled slowly out, with me close behind.

Fritz cried, I cried when we said farewell at the door of the black Lincoln his wife had hired to take him home. He gave me a one-armed hug, the other arm being still in the grey sling, and then from his shirt pocket he fished out a small square of paper with something he had drawn in pencil, a round figure with some straight-line geometry within it. "This may help you out someday," he said. "I signed it." Actually I loved this memento. I took the drawing home with me that evening, and used it as a special bookmark from then on. It kept my thoughts in the proper place for years. But eventually I lost track of which book I had left the drawing in.

Well, years after completing my hospital obligation I had gone on to make my livelihood by writing. By 1969 I had landed a regular job as a copy boy at Time Magazine. Before long I was getting simple writing assignments, so I kept up with reading things like the New York Times obituary section. One morning I was fumbling through the obits looking for a possible story when I was saddened to come upon a two column death notice with the name of my old painter friend with the tweed cap, Fritz Glarner.

Why, I wondered, would Fritz get an obit in the world's great newspaper of record? But then as I read I learned that he was no garage painter. His paintings hung in museums, in the Met, and side by side with the priceless Mondrians at the Museum of Modern Art. Piet Mondrian, the obit said, had been Fritz's inspiration and best friend in the art world. I shrank in my own skin when I remembered how I had lectured to him about Mondrian! I could just see his amused but loving expression.

The obituary's list of works by Fritz also included mention of a Glarner mural in the Time-Life building in Rockefeller Center, which of course was the building in which I was sitting at that moment, and like a gong I realized that it could only refer to the huge mural that I passed by twice every day on my way to and from work– that vast, bright and busy mural that was, yes, reminiscent of Mondrian. Better, maybe. Deeper down.

I folded the newspaper and rushed to the down elevators. The security guard in the foyer, who knew me by sight, saw me staring at the mural and came over to ask what I was doing. I told him of Glarner's death. We both looked up at the mural as if an image of Fritz himself could be distinguished among the geometries. The guard asked if I knew the story. "What story?" He told me that Glarner had once owed considerable money to his patrons, the Rockefeller family, money he could not repay, so he had agreed to create a mural for this new Rockefeller Center in lieu of payment. There were other works and designs too.

The guard seemed to know what he was talking about. He told me a Glarner's mural could also be seen in the United Nations General Assembly, so a few minutes later I was on my way out the revolving door and rushing across town to see that wonderful painting as well. It still stands, twenty-four feet tall, in the Dag Hammerskjold Library. It probably always will.

In those days I was making very little money with my reporting and writing, even at Time, and it was not lost on me as I tracked down famous works by Fritz Glarner that somewhere at home was a book, with my place marked by an original work of art signed by him. I had always treasured it, simply because Fritz had kindly presented it to me and I had liked him so much. But now I went uptown in a different set of mind to look at the catalogue of the Metropolitan Museum for works by Glarner, and yes, they had several in their permanent collection. They were mostly small pencil sketches.

I was suddenly afflicted by an unwanted sense of avarice and suspicion. Back home I wanted to shake out every book I had, but quick rifflings of many pages soon slowed down to a long, tedious page-by-page search that eventually took me back through every one of my books. The avarice subsided as the search went on, because I was getting sidetracked, the search was forcing me to revisit not only where I had been when I acquired each book, but also to re-imagine the lives I had lived vicariously through my readings... Lafcadio's Adventures, George Fox's Journals...each book brought something vivid back to the fore. The search was taking weeks, then months. Eventually I almost forgot what I was looking for.

For years I would not throw away any book because I might have overlooked the page in which the priceless missing sketch was wedged. But then, if I found it, would I be able to bring myself to sell it? Why would I ever need so much money? So even in its odd disappearance, or perhaps because of it, Fritz's simple gift kept provoking big questions and enriching my life. Every now and then I look at my shelves of classic books collected over fifty years, and think that I may yet find my fortune there, the hope of which - not the finding - is the true value of any lost and buried treasure.

. . .

# Two Ways to Catch a Thief

Eleanor Roosevelt helped found the Wiltwyck School for a hundred delinquent boys in Esopus New York, where I worked for many years. She put on an annual picnic for all the boys over at Valkill, her estate in Hyde Park, almost directly across the Hudson River from the stone buildings of the school. Yellow buses would pull up on big day to drive the kids across the bridge to Poughkeepsie and then north to Hyde Park. They would not come back until late, the kids covered with bramble scratches, their shoes and pants cuffs wet, stomachs full of satisfaction and hot dogs.

One year, though, shortly after the buses returned to campus from the picnic, the Director of the school received a call from Mrs. Roosevelt herself. "It seems my ring of keys disappeared today," she said.

The director was horrified. He would find the keys immediately, he said. He would have all the boys lined up and searched at once. The thief would be punished.

The phone was briefly silent. "Well, if you wouldn't mind," said Mrs. Roosevelt, "I'd rather invite the boys back tomorrow for another picnic. To help me look for the keys."

And my last story is about a question posed by Duty Hall, a ninety year old Quaker who told our children a story each week when we were gathered in the simple Meeting House out on Plutarch road, seated in a circle in an old wooden room, sun streaming through the plain glass windows, the children waiting like the rest of us in expectant silence. If someone wanted to speak they spoke. If someone wanted to sing, they sang. There was no organ. Old Duty, with his full shock of white hair, wore his usual jeans, denim jacket, and work boots to Meeting. He carried no Bible. He simply stood up when he was ready, and began speaking. His messages often urged us to be patient in adversity, thankful in prosperity. On one particular June day when the fruit trees were in blossom he stood and told a story for the children.

"This place used to be a farm house," he said, "built by a Dutch carpenter. He lived here with his family. There used to be a big old pear tree, right there outside that window. It was their pride and joy because it gave so many juicy pears." Some children scooted a little closer to hear the teller.

"Well, one night the carpenter was lying here in the house, asleep beside his wife, when all of a sudden he woke up because he had heard a cracking noise outside. Quietly he crept over to look out the window, and there, up above, he saw by the moonlight that there was a big raggedy man, a thief, climbing around and breaking branches up in the tree. Well of course by then his wife had woken up too, and the family's three little daughters, Grce, Helen and Marion, also heard the noise, and crept barefoot into the parents bedroom."

The children in the Meeting House looked out the window as if the tree and the thief were still there. Duty glanced at each of them and asked, "What do you think the carpenter decided to do about it?"

They pondered, hesitated, and then guessed: "Did he yell at the thief to go away?" asked one boy.

"No," said Duty.

"Did he call the police?" asked another.

"No, dear, there were no telephones back then," said Duty. "They had to solve the problem themselves. The thief was right up there, stealing their pears, making noise, breaking branches…"

"I know!" offered an urgent boy, stretching his hand up, "I think the farmer went and loaded his shotgun!"

Duty shook his head. "Oh, my goodness no, we don't shoot people!" He waited a while longer. "Well, I suppose some of you want to know what the carpenter really did do?" Yes, please, they would like to know the answer, right now.

"All right. He told his oldest daughter to go get the tallest ladder and stand it up against the tree." Duty sat down.

The children of the meeting looked at each other as if Duty were crazy, but their eyes showed that they knew a moral was coming. Finally one of the girls surrendered. "Okay," she asked, "why did he want her to go get a ladder?"

Duty smiled, having caught them in his trap. "He wanted them to put the ladder up there so the thief wouldn't hurt himself when he came down!

*Work, for the night is coming!*
*Work through the sunny noon;*
*Fill brightest hours with labor,*
*Rest comes sure and soon.*
*Give every flying minute,*
*Something to keep in store;*
*Work, for the night is coming,*
*When we will work no more.*

Traditional Hymn by Anna Coghill, 1854
(Sung at my grandfather's piano, 1945)

## First Readers' Reviews

"These tales may be seen as in the same vein as Wendell Berry's country stories. Schoonbeck's observations, dry and laconic, are emotional too, with turns of phrase that ground you suddenly in reality -- actual reminiscence rather than created tales. *"But now he was sitting here in Spanish Moss cracker-house Florida, among egrets and manatees, drinking a cup of coffee."* Scenes of pleasant, deadpan absurdity... his observations arise perhaps from the distance at which society held him much of his life."

Josiah Dearborn
Cannondale, Connecticut

"This and all of his stories are a gold mine of geographical and psychological trajectory and discovery, ever asking us to consider our personal, political, and civic purpose.

Susan Casey Vinett
*Vassar College Bookstore*

Once again, tales that are intriguing and thought provoking.

-Sue Tebbe
New Orleans, Louisiana